ALLURING SURRENDER

Book 5 Bayou Stix

By

SKYE TURNER

Alluring Surrender
Book 5 Bayou Stix
By
Skye Turner
****
Print Edition
****

The author acknowledges the real people or places and copyrighted or trademarked status and trademark owners of the following wordmarks mentioned in this work of fiction: Abita Pecan Harvest Ale, Afghanistan, Alexander McQueen, Atchafalaya Basin, Batman, Baton Rouge, Baton Rouge Halloween Parade, Black Widow, Captain America, Christian Louboutin, Cinclaire, Community Coffee Pumpkin Praline, Director Fury, Fireball, Flo Jo, Froot Loops, Gabbie Duran, Highway 1, Hocus Pocus, Hummer, Ice Queen, Kindle, Les Miles, Louisiana, LSU, Nerf, Netflix, No White Flags, Robin, Splenda, Steve Gleason, Superman, Team Gleason, TMZ, Twilight, Usain Bolt, West Baton Rouge, Walk-Ons.

Cover Design by: Kari Ayasha of Cover to Cover Designs
www.covertocoverdesigns.com

Cover Photography: Michael Meadows Studios/ Michael Meadows
www.michaelmeadowsstudios.com

Cover Models: Jamaal Lewis and Taryn Horn

Editor: Mandy Schoen www.mandyschoenedits.com

Formatting: BB eBooks Thailand/ Paul Salvette bbebooksthailand.com

Author Bio Photography: Rich Roth www.richroth.net

*Due to graphic sex scenes and strong language, this book is not intended for readers under the age of 18. This is an ADULT book and contains graphic sex scenes and explicit language. It also contains delicate topics that may be hard for sensitive readers to handle.

Dedication

This book is dedicated to everyone who's ever had

someone look down on them.

YOU define YOU. The only way others can is if you

give them the power.

Dream big. Be true to you.

Define yourself!

Acknowledgements

Thank you to my amazeballs Beta readers: Betsy Whitley, *Cover to Cover Book Blog,* Joely Bogan, Kristin Blay, Lindsey Lawson, Noelle Riviere, Stephanie Dillander, Thomas Noble, and Tiffany Tyler, *Reading in Black and White.*

Thank you Kari Ayasha of **Cover to Cover Designs** for once more giving me EXACTLY what I wanted! You are a rock star babe!

Thank you to Michael Meadows of *Michael Meadows Studios* for the awesome cover photography.

THANK YOU to my awesome readers and Street Team, Bayou Belle's and Beau's! Love y'all for loving me and my characters!

For my other amazingly supportive bestie author/blogger friends, thanks for being awesome. Ma Boo-TH Snyder, JM Witt, LL Collins, Kathy Coopmans, Joanne Schwehm, Gabbie Duran, SK Hartley, AD Justice, Jamie Whitley, and so, so many more.

And finally, but most importantly… *Thank you to my awesome, sexy, supportive husband, James, and the two perfect little hellions we created together. Writing is my job and my passion, but you three are my WORLD.*

Books by Skye Turner

BAYOU STIX SERIES

Alluring Turmoil, Book 1 Bayou Stix

Alluring Seduction, Book 2 Bayou Stix

Alluring Ties, A Bayou Stix Novella, Book 2.5 Bayou Stix

Alluring Temptation, Book 3 Bayou Stix

Alluring Infatuation, Book 4 Bayou Stix

Chapter One

Cruz

"Are you going to see Tifanie tonight?"

I sigh as I look around Java and Sweeties and I try to avoid Jude's question. It's packed today. There isn't an empty table, chair, or couch in the entire place. Luckily, since Jude is married to the owner of the most popular coffee shop/bakery in Baton Rouge, we never have to worry about having a place to sit here. We kind of have a "reserved" table in the corner by the huge windows.

A kick under the table alerts me to the fact that I am not going to be able to ignore the question. I look up into the grinning face of Jessie. "So, are you seeing the hot paramedic tonight, Cruz?"

I shrug. "I don't know. We don't typically make plans to hang out in advance."

I don't like talking about this. Tifanie and I have been hanging out for a couple of months now. We're friends and we have good conversation and laughs together. She's sexy as hell but I just don't... we're friends.

A throat clears and I look into Dade's curious brown eyes as he stares at me. "You seem to hang out a lot lately."

I shrug again. "Yeah, she's pretty fun."

Jessie chuckles. "She's fun?! No, she's *fine*. With a capital 'F.' Have you tapped that yet?"

I glare at him and grip the table top to stop from punching my friend in the face. Jude smacks him in the back of the head and mutters, "Don't be a crude ass, Jessie!"

Jessie rubs the back of his head and smirks. "I wasn't. I was just trying to get a rise out of him." He nods in my direction and I can see Dade smile. "He just seems to be spending an awful lot of time with *fun* Tifanie lately."

"Why do you need to get a rise out of me?" I ask.

Jessie laughs. "Because dude, she's *FINE* and she wants you. Yet, you don't seem to be willing to make a move!"

I mutter under my breath, "Yeah, well…"

He needs to mind his own business.

Liam nods at me. "What's the deal, Cruz?"

Why are they so damn curious about my life?! It's not like that with Tifanie and me.

"It's not even like that. We're just friends. We hang out and have fun. Stop making it more than it is. We're just friends."

Jessie laughs. "Right." He drags the word out. "So, who are you trying to convince of that, man?"

"Screw you. It's not like that!"

Dammit… it's *not* like that. We're *just* friends. It's all we can be. Tifanie is sexy and sweet; she doesn't press me and we have a good time. She's easy to talk to and I enjoy her company, but I can't… no, I *won't* go there with her.

Even though she fills out a pair of jeans like a dream. Dammit, stop thinking about her ass in her jeans, Cruz! She's your friend.

3

You're her friend. That's it. That's all it is. Friends. Even though she seems to occupy a little too much of your mind lately.

No, fuck that. We're friends. It's all we can be.

Dade is being Dade and watching my face. He sees I notice and he winks at me. I mutter under my breath and look away.

He laughs out loud.

Jude diverts everyone's attention from me by leaning forward and asking about Clove, Liam's wife and Dade's baby sister. "How's she doing with the bed rest? Lexi says she's miserable being confined to a bed." He seems really interested in the answer.

Liam grimaces. "Yeah, it's not fun. She hates being on bed rest. All she can do is stay in bed except when she has to go to the bathroom, but we have to keep him in there for a bit longer. They say if we can make it another few weeks, we'll be good."

Clove is a good friend. We've been friends since we were kids and now she's married to one of my best friends and

4

band mates. They are great together, but I am worried about her. Not because she's married to Liam; he adores her. But, she's had a rough couple of months with her pregnancy.

Jude sighs. "We're all hoping for that and I'm hoping we don't have to deal with bed rest with our own baby, though that morning sickness shit is no joke either." He shrugs sheepishly and looks at Liam. "No offense, dude."

Liam chuckles. "None taken. I hope Lexi has smooth sailing."

Jessie interrupts, "Yeah well, can we stop all the baby talk?" He rubs the back of his neck and pulls his lip ring into his mouth. He always does that when he's antsy. He mutters, "I'm not ready to deal with all that yet. Don't give me the water you two are drinking!"

I laugh at him. "Jessie, I don't think the world is ready for any little Jessies right now anyway!"

A laugh at the tableside draws everyone's attention. We look up into the sparkling eyes of Blue, Jessie's fiancée. "Yes, no babies yet! My man-child is all I can handle right now."

She fakes a shudder. "God, don't curse me with another one of him."

Jessie mutters, "Hey, woman! I'm fucking amazing. But, yeah, when we make babies, I want a mini-Blue so I can kick some boys' asses when she gets older! For now though, we can keep practicing. Three to four times a day!"

We all laugh as Blue grabs his face and kisses him.

Coffees are delivered to the table and our publicist, Bradi, sits down. "Ok, boys. Let's get down to business. Enough baby talk since Micah and I don't have any... yet!" She laughs, but then gets right to it and we go over the schedule for the arena tour we'll be starting in about eight weeks.

We're wrapping up the meeting when my cell buzzes with a new text.

"Tifanie:

Pizza and beer tonight at Walk-Ons to watch the LSU game?"

I look up and see Jessie laughing at me. "So, having *fun*

with legs tonight?"

Blue glares at him. "Why exactly are you noticing Tifanie's legs?"

He blows her a kiss. "Because they are long and shapely." She frowns. "Simmer down, woman! I prefer your legs. They *are* attached to that fabulous ass I'm so fond of."

She laughs and presses a quick kiss to his neck as she squirms out of his lap. "You are incorrigible, Jessie Adams!"

He grins and pops her ass as she stands up. "Yup. You love it!" He wiggles his eyebrows and pulls on his lip ring.

She rolls her eyes as she walks away. "True story!" She wiggles her fingers at us as she disappears into the kitchen.

Bradi stands up and calls over her shoulder as she also heads toward the kitchen. "Y'all behave." She winks at me and smirks. "And Cruz, have fun with Tifanie tonight!"

What the hell?! Everyone is out to get me. They all have the wrong idea about Tifanie and me. Way wrong. We're just going to watch the game. That's it!

I sigh as I text her back to tell her I'm in. I see everyone smirking at me as I type. I flip them off.

Chapter Two

Tifanie

God, what a long twenty-four hours it's been! Is there a full moon tonight? We've dealt with nothing but crazy people today.

Luckily, a gorgeous man kept me sane. Well, not him, but thinking about him and his haunted blue eyes did.

Ha, you're an idiot, Tifanie. Cruz has never so much as made a move on you.

He's interested. I can see he's interested, but he won't make a move. Why not?

We hang out all the time. We spend a lot of time together, yet, he's never even kissed me.

There's something that's holding him back, but damned if I know what it is. I'm just being patient and biding my time. He'll act on it. He has to… right?!

Because I am aching with the need to kiss him.

Good lord, I'm an idiot. I'm twenty-five years old and mooning over a man who is scared of me. Yet, something pulls me to him; so I wait… I'll wait.

Ty, my partner, breaks me out of my musings as I stare sightlessly at the TV in the station. "Earth to Tif." He snaps his fingers in my face and I shake my head to clear it as I look at him. "Yo, wake up. Only a few more hours to go. You thinking about the brooding drummer?"

I frown at his description of Cruz. "I'm awake. And he's not brooding, but yes, busted. I was thinking about him."

Ty smiles slightly at me. "Ok. Perhaps brooding is the wrong word. Wounded, maybe?!"

I grimace. There's truth to that statement. "That one might work…"

He chuckles. "So, what's the latest?"

I click my tongue as I think about how to answer him.

"Well, there is no latest. It's pretty much the same. Nothing new to report."

He stares at me and arches a brow. "Nothing new to report? You've been spending time with him for almost two months and there's nothing to report?!" He looks at me incredulously. "Are you kidding me?" He mumbles, but I catch it. "He's an idiot."

I shrug. "Yeah, nothing new. We hang out. We do things together, but we're just friends. He doesn't seem to want to change the equation." I smile, though it bothers me. "What can I say? Maybe he's just not that into me. At least as anything other than a buddy."

Ty laughs. "Yeah, ok. I'm calling bullshit on that one. Have you seen you? No straight man wants to be just friends with you, Tif. Is he gay?"

That makes me laugh. *Is Cruz gay? Um, no. I've seen the hungry look in his eyes when he thinks I'm not paying attention. He's not gay. He's interested, but why won't he act on it? What's the deal?*

I say out loud, "He's *not* gay. And you're straight."

Ty makes a face at me. "I am definitely straight! Tif, I don't want to see you hurt. You're an amazing woman and you care about the drummer. But, I care about you and I don't want to see you with a broken heart. I'll kick his ass if that happens."

He would too. Ty has been my partner for two years now. He's a great guy. We are like brother and sister though; so the fact that he's completely hot, while not lost on me, does nothing for me. That would be gross.

I pat his cheek. "I know you would. I love you for it, too; but I can take care of myself. I'm a big girl. We're friends, Ty. I'm giving him space and time to realize how awesome I am. And he will. He has to, right?!"

He kisses my palm and bites it. "He better. Or he really is a fucking idiot!" He laughs as I jerk my hand away and punch his shoulder. As he rubs it, he asks, "So, want to head to Walk-Ons to catch the game tonight or are you just going to head home and go to bed?"

I'd forgotten a pre-season football game was on tonight.

I'm exhausted from the crazy calls with our shift, but I nod as I check my phone. Ty laughs at me. "Go ahead. Ask him if he wants to come too. Maybe I can be your wingman!"

I roll my eyes at Ty, but laugh. "My wingman?"

He nods. "Yup. I'll throw some meat your way to see how he reacts. I'll help you land him."

I chuckle as I think it through. *What would it hurt? I can flirt with a few people and just see how Cruz reacts. If he really isn't interested, then he won't care, but if he IS, he'll let me know. Two months is long enough to figure it out. I've made it more than clear that I'm interested.*

If this little nudge is what it takes, then bring it on.

I nod. "Ok, Robin. Let's do this!"

He grins and I don't mistake the twinkle in his eyes. *Oh lord, I hope this doesn't backfire!* But he gripes with a smile. "Why am I Robin? I want to be Batman! You look better in tights!"

Grinning, I wink. "Truth. But both wear tights." I text Cruz and within minutes he texts back saying he'll meet us there tonight at six.

Leaning back against the seat, I take a deep breath.

Ty pats my hand. "Tif, in all seriousness… if he's interested, you'll know. I just don't want you to be unsure anymore."

Turning my head, I smile at Ty and take him in. His chestnut hair has auburn highlights and he has sage-colored eyes. He's fair skinned, but he tans and works out five days a week as well as plays flag football whenever he can; so he's fit. He's the best.

He sees my inspection. "Why are you looking at me like that? You're creeping me out."

Grinning, I lick my lips and I outright laugh as he fidgets uncomfortably on the seat. "When are you going to get a steady woman, Ty?"

He drums his fingers on the door as he stares out of the window. "I don't know. When one makes me want to, I guess."

I cluck my tongue. "And you think you're going to find a

worthwhile one in the bar sluts you bring home every night?"

He looks at me and scowls. "When did this conversation become about me?! I thought we were talking about the drummer."

"Oh you know, diversion…"

He laughs as he tweaks my nose. Dispatch comes over the radio at that moment with a call. *"Possible cardiac arrest. Male, thirty-eight, was involved in rigorous intercourse and started having chest pains. Unable to catch his breath. Lips are blue…"*

Ty looks at me. "Ok, let's do this. Let's go save a life."

He heads to the ambulance, while I radio dispatch to get the exact location. Ty drives as I check over my bag and put Cruz into the back of my mind. My adrenaline starts pumping as I mentally prepare myself for whatever awaits us at the location.

Two hours later our shift is over and we are heading out of the station after showering and changing clothes. I feel amazing. We did indeed save the gentleman's life.

Ty is waiting in the hall as I exit the women's locker room. He straightens up from the wall. "So, you ready for beer and wings?"

I link my arm with his as we stroll outside. "I am. Ready to decompress."

He stops at his truck. "Want to ride with me? That way Cruz can bring you home?" He waggles his eyebrows as he says it.

Pursing my lips as I tap my foot, I nod. "Yes."

He laughs as he opens my door and bends down in an exaggerated bow. "Your carriage, my lady."

I snicker at his absurdity. "You're ridiculous."

He grins as he shuts the door and swivels his hips to a beat only he can hear as he rounds the truck. Within minutes, we're heading to campus. "There's a table for us. Some of the guys have been drinking since noon, so I'm sure they're already tanked, but at least we'll have a table!"

"Shit, I didn't even think about that." I totally forgot it was game day and Walk-Ons was on campus. "I should text

Cruz, too."

Ty glances over at me. "Take a picture of your boobs and send it to him."

"WHAT?!"

He laughs. "Why are you acting so shocked? Your boobs look great in that shirt. It's sexy. You look sexy, so send him a picture."

"I can't… I won't… I'm not doing that!"

We stop at a red light and he looks at me. "Why not? You want him to know you want more, right?" He glances at my cleavage. "Trust me, sending him a picture of your tits will work to your advantage!"

I roll my eyes at him. "He doesn't care about my tits!"

"Bullshit! If he's not gay, he cares about your tits!"

"Are we seriously having a conversation about my boobs, Ty?! And he's *not* gay!"

I can't send Cruz a picture of my cleavage. He would flip out. On the other hand… I can send him a picture of my shirt! I had a fitted LSU shirt in my locker. I can send him the photo and just act oblivious. If my girls look fabulous in it, well, that can be an added perk.

Holding out my camera, I pull the scoop neck down just a little more and smile for the camera as I snap the selfie.

Ty laughs. "Let me see!" I hold the phone out and show him. "Mmmmmm hmmmmm. Perfect. Send that."

Before I chicken out, I type a quick message and hit send, then place the phone on my lap and close my eyes with my head back on the seat.

Traffic is crazy getting into campus, so I'm glad Ty is driving, allowing me to rest my eyes for a bit. I'm tired. Today was a long day. Thankfully, we're off tomorrow and I can catch up on my sleep.

I must have fallen asleep. I'm startled as Ty gently shakes me as he calls my name. "Tifanie. Wake up, doll. We're here."

Sitting up, I stretch. "Thanks, Ty. Sorry. I fell asleep."

He chuckles and smirks at me. "You did. It's ok. It was only for about twenty minutes." He slaps my thigh. "Now wake your ass up! Time to get you some!"

I laugh as I open the door. "You're a fool, Ty!"

He laughs as we head into the noise coming out of the sports bar.

Chapter Three

Cruz

---

*S*he sent me a picture. Why did she send me a photo? And her shirt is VERY low in it. She's wearing that tonight? Why would she send me a photo? She's never done that before.

Her text was weird. The text was normal, but the photo was not. She's making me insane. I don't know how to handle this. All it said was, *"Geaux Tigers!"* But why the picture?

I'm trying to decipher the meaning as I navigate through all of the traffic getting to campus. My radio is loud, though I don't even know what song is on. I'm so deep into my thoughts.

I couldn't fathom a response to the picture, so I didn't

respond. I'll be there in five minutes anyway.

My phone rings as I hit the gates of LSU. Glancing at the caller ID, I see "Momma" on the display. Hitting the button on the dashboard to connect the call, I answer, "Hey, Momma. What's going on? Everything ok?"

"Hey, baby. Everything is fine. I was just calling to check in with you. I haven't talked to you in a few days."

Drumming my fingers on the steering wheel, I reply, "Things have been a little busy. We've been having a lot of band meetings and Bradi is keeping us hopping to prepare for the arena tour in about two months. Why they decided to start the tour around Thanksgiving is beyond me. She's been frantically scheduling all these interviews and photo shoots. Sorry I haven't called you. How are you? How is everything going?"

She sighs. "Everything is going fine, baby. I just wanted to hear your voice. It's been a trying time."

I grip the wheel tightly. "I know, Momma. Has he contacted you again?"

She's quiet for a bit, then she answers, "Yes. He's called a few times, but I just let the machine get it. I don't want you to worry. He can't hurt me. He says he just wants to talk and to apologize."

My vision is red with the fury in my mind. How dare that son of a bitch call my momma? Taking a deep breath, I try to control my rage. "Do you want me to call his parole officer? I can handle this. Don't talk to him. Seriously, Momma. Don't talk to him."

I can hear her hand shaking through the car speakers. "Cruz, baby, I didn't call you to upset you. You're a good son. I love you so much. But, I don't want you to stress about this. I just wanted to hear my strong boy's voice. You always brighten my day. You brighten my life. I'm not worrying about him and you shouldn't either. You don't have to call his parole officer. I have the number, too. That's not why I called you. I don't need you to protect me, baby." I hear the road noise. "Where are you headed tonight?"

"I love you, too, Momma. I know you don't *need* me to

protect you, but I'm your son and I'm going to do whatever I can to make your life easier. I owe you that after everything you've done for me my whole life. You night not need me to handle things, but that doesn't mean I don't want to.

"Anyway, I'm actually going to watch the LSU game with some friends. I'm heading to campus to meet them and traffic is ridiculous."

She laughs softly. "I know that. You're a good son. The best and I love you. You're my precious baby, even as a grown man that women fawn over.

"Well, it's obviously not the band you're meeting with. You would have said you were meeting the guys. Are you meeting that girl you've been spending so much time with? The one I'm not allowed to ask about?"

Great. I should have known she'd pick up on that. I don't want to get her hopes up. "Yes, I'm meeting Tifanie. But, don't overthink this. She's a friend."

I hear her sigh again. "I'm not overthinking anything. I just want you to keep your head and heart open. You deserve to be happy and find you a good woman, baby. That's all I'm saying about it. She seems to have something you find interesting since you spend so much time with her lately. Just don't stop something before it can start. Promise me that?!"

What is she talking about? I'm not stopping anything. We really are *just* friends. But I hear myself say, "Yes, Ma'am. I promise," as I pull into the packed lot and look for a spot to park.

I see a truck leaving in the back so I navigate the people spilling over into the parking lot and head toward it. As I throw it into park, I say, "Well, Momma, I'm here. I need to get inside. Kick-off is in about half an hour. I'm going to come by tomorrow, ok?"

"Ok, baby. Plan on staying for dinner tomorrow night. Have fun. And keep an open mind. I love you."

"Love you too, Momma. I'll be there tomorrow. Good-night."

She says the same and I un-sync the phone and adjust my

cap as I head into the noise of the bar.

I walk in and look around as my eyes adjust to the lighting. I see Tifanie and her coworker, Ty, at the bar getting drinks. She looks good.

As if she knows I'm there, she turns and smiles at me. I see Ty lean down and say something into her ear. She shakes her head and laughs at him. My stomach clenches with surprising jealousy.

Stop it. Shake it off. Friends… just friends.

She nods her head toward the far corner of the bar area where I see a rowdy bunch at a table and holds a beer up. I nod in agreement and make my way through the large crowd, all the while keeping my gaze on her backside. I'm stopped a few times and drunk girls and guys ask me if I'm, well me, but I smile and shake my head to deny it. I hate being recognized and having people focus on me.

As I get closer to the table, I see Tifanie talking to a burly guy with a LSU cap on. Ty has his arm thrown across the guy's shoulders and I catch the tail end of the conversation as I approach. "…single and ready to mingle. You know she loves seafood and there are several places in town she likes. Maybe y'all can do something tomorrow. We are off."

What? Is she interested in him? Is he asking her out?

She chuckles and looks over at me with her eyes full of mirth, but she looks tired. Her face lights up and my chest swells. "Hey, Cruz. You made it."

I nod and incline my head to Ty and his *buddy*. "I did. Traffic is a bitch out there."

Ty laughs. "Yeah it is. It's campus and a game night. How's it going, man?"

"Good. Busy." I know I seem short, but I don't talk to people. And I don't think he likes me anyway.

He clicks his tongue and stares at me before smirking and turning back to his friend and Tif. They talk and Tif looks at me with a smile. "Hey, handsome. I got you a beer. Abita Pecan Harvest Ale is on draft."

Ah, Abita. I do love this Louisiana beer. I take it from her as she holds it out and our hands brush. Ignoring the charge racing up my arm, I take a quick gulp. This is getting more and more difficult every day.

She takes a sip and looks at me over the rim of her glass. Finally I can't take it and mutter, "What?"

She leans over to be heard above the noise of the bar and says into my ear, "You ok?"

I immediately nod, though her perception makes me nervous. She smiles and says, "Ok, you don't have to tell me, but I'm here if you want to." Linking her arm with mine, she pulls me closer toward the table and two empty stools. "Hey guys! Look who decided to join us."

The table is full of paramedics and firemen. I've seen them a few times over the past couple of months, so I'm not as uncomfortable. Though I'm not on friendly terms with any of them and Tifanie is the only female in the bunch. Several nod at me through alcohol-glazed eyes and I notice that Ty and his friend are both looking at Tifanie and me and our linked arms. The friend is scowling.

Not my issue, dude.

The evening goes off without a hitch as we watch the game. I nurse the one beer, since I never drink and drive, while Tif has a couple and LSU wins over Wisconsin. As the place erupts in cheers and cat-calls, Tifanie hops off the stool she's been occupying and says she's going to the restroom.

I nod as I watch the announcers interview Les Miles on the large screen and pop a fried pickle into my mouth. I'm not much for conversation with people I'm not really close to and most of these guys are drunk and trying to pick up the cute waitresses serving us.

Tifanie's stool is pulled out and Ty sits down. I notice his friend isn't at the table anymore. I look at Ty because it's obvious he wants to talk to me. My brow arches.

He chuckles and takes a sip of his beer. "So, what's the deal, Drummer Boy?"

"What deal?"

"You know what I'm talking about. You're not an idiot. Or are you?!"

29

What the hell? Is everyone going to get on my case today about this? I just look at him and answer dryly, "Not sure what you're getting at, Ty."

"Yeah, ok. I'll spell it out for you. You and Tifanie. What's the deal? Are you interested in her or not?"

"What's it to you?" I ask.

He stares at me and shakes his head. "She's my partner. I care about her. We're friends and she's like family. She's into you. You're not an idiot. You have to know that. Yet, you hang out with her and nothing happens. I think you're an ok dude, but if you aren't interested in her, back off. Either make a move or walk away."

Is this asshole threatening me? Who does he think he is? Tifanie and I are friends. Just friends. I respect her and we have a good time. I like her, but this guy is not going to tell me what to do. It's none of his business.

I breathe through my nose and look at him. "I respect your opinion. You're her partner and I get that you're looking out for her, but we're friends. What happens with us is our business."

He nods and chuckles. "All I'm saying is shit or get off the pot, Drummer Boy. In case you haven't noticed, she's hot. But I know you've noticed. I see you noticing. Lots of people notice. So, if you don't figure it out and fast, someone else is going to take your shot." He stands up and taps the table. "Like Remy." He nods toward the bathrooms where I see Tifanie talking to his friend. Their heads are close together and they're laughing. Her cheeks are flushed and his hands are resting comfortably on her shoulders.

My hands clench and my jaw locks. He smirks as he throws his hands up. "Take the shot..." and walks away.

I'm left sitting at the table watching Tifanie flirt with Remy and an unwanted feeling in my gut.

Son of a bitch... What am I going to do here? Am I going to take a chance and make a move or am I going to walk away?

Dammit, why does this have to be so complicated? There are just so many things that she doesn't know. So many things I haven't told her. I haven't told anyone. No one knows. Except the guys and girls. Am I ready to let someone in?

Weirdly, I think I want to let Tifanie in. I just hope she doesn't walk away once she knows the facts…

What do I do here?

Chapter Four

Tifanie

Remy is so attractive and sweet. He's flirting like crazy and we've had a casual thing when he's been home on leave in the past, but I'm so focused on Cruz at the table with Ty that I'm not giving Remy the attention he deserves. He chuckles as he notices my distraction.

"You're not here with me, are you?"

I shake my head and smile at him. "I'm sorry. I am here and I like you. You know that."

He nods and grimaces. "I do. But you like the drummer more."

I swallow and glance over at Cruz. He's looking over here, but looks away as soon as our eyes meet. Returning my gaze to Remy, I shrug. "I'm sorry. He's worked his way under my skin."

His eyes search mine and he smiles sadly. "I see that. He seems ok, but he's got something going on, Tif. Just be careful. I like you and we've had fun. I'm home now and I've thought about possibly starting something up… with you… but, I see the coy glances you throw his way. You and me… we've had a good time. But you," he inclines his chin toward Cruz, "and him, well, I can't compete with that. Just be careful."

I smile at Remy and lean up to kiss his cheek. Leaning back, I cup his face. "I'm sorry." He smiles sadly at me. "I know he has stuff going on. I'd like for him to share that stuff with me." I sigh. "I'm just not sure he ever will."

He tucks my hair behind my ear. "If the covert glances are an indication, he will."

Looking back at Cruz, I see Ty get up from the table and stroll away. Cruz looks back at me and this time, he stares. He swallows and I can see his throat working. My gut clenches at the sight and I let out an unintentional sigh.

Remy chuckles. "Ok, then. Go on girl, go break that man down." He gives me a wink and walks in the same direction Ty just went.

I continue to stare at Cruz. Neither of us is willing to be the first to look away this time. When my insides are a complete puddle of mush and my panties are completely soaked, I take a deep breath and look away. Then, straightening my back, I head back to the blue eyes at the table.

He watches me walk. As I reach the table, I swipe his beer since mine is empty and take a swig of the warm liquid before sitting down on my stool. Turning to him, I smile. He's watching me warily. Leaning over, I decide to push the envelope. I want him. And it's time to step up my game.

His eyes widen as I encroach on his space, but he holds firm. Leaning in, I stop at the shell of his ear. "You ready to get out of here? I'm beat and I need a ride home. Take me?"

He pulls back slightly and watches me. I hold my breath. He nods and stands up.

My breath whooshes out as he turns his back to leave. He doesn't move though. He just stands there. Finally, he turns around and holds his hand out to help me down. Not that he needs to. Without a second thought, I place my hand in his and he doesn't drop it as we walk out of the bar into the night.

We walk to his car in comfortable silence as he continues to lightly hold my hand. As we stop at the passenger door, I make no move to open it. He quirks his brow as I stare at him and he leans down, boxing me in as he opens it. I refuse to move and I can feel his accelerated breaths against my neck. I stare at him, willing him to look at me. He exhales and turns his head. Our faces are so close I can see the darker rim of blue around his startlingly light eyes in his caramel face. Without thinking it through, I lightly brush my lips against his full, perfect ones. Just once. Then, I duck under his arm and plop onto the seat because my knees are so weak, I'm about to collapse.

He stands there for a full minute before closing the door

and walking around to his side of the car. He opens the door and sits in silence before starting the car. The engine roars and it makes me jump.

Staring ahead, he calmly asks, "Why did you do that?"

I lean my head back and angle my body toward his as I sigh. "Because I wanted to, Cruz."

He swallows and turns his head, looking at me. "You do whatever you want to do?"

I laugh. "Not all the time. If I did, I'd have kissed you long before now. But yes, I do for the most part."

He chuckles lightly too. "Ok."

Just "ok?" I finally kiss him, sort of. After two months, I finally decide to just do what I want and his response is "ok?"

Shit, I've already crossed the threshold, so I'm just going for it! He's going to either admit he's interested or not, but I'm tired of dancing around this shit.

I want him. I am pretty certain he wants me, so tonight, Cruz Edwards, tonight you're making a choice. Either you're interested or you're not, but tonight, tonight, you're making a choice!

Dear God, let it be the choice I want you to make though.

"What does 'ok' mean?"

He looks at me in confusion. "What does it mean?!"

I stare at him and take a deep breath. "Yes, what does it mean? I kissed you. Finally. I'm going to be straight with you so you can't say you don't know what it is I want. I want *you*!" His eyes go wide at my point blank declaration. "I like you. I want to date you. I want you, Cruz. I'm interested in you on so many levels. I think you want me too, yet, you're scared or unwilling to make the first move, so I'm making it for you.

"I want you. That's what I want. If you don't want me in the same way, I'll stop this. We can go back to being friends and just hanging out, but I'm tired of this dance. If you want me, take me. I'm here. If you don't, it's totally ok. It'll suck for a bit, but I'm a big girl. So, you know what I want. The question now is what do *you* want?"

He stares at me and his intense gaze searches my face before he groans and looks out of his window. I watch his reflection in the glass as he closes his eyes and takes a deep breath. His eyes meet mine through the reflection. I don't look away. I refuse to look away.

Finally, he says something. "It's complicated, Tifanie."

Without thinking, I grab his arm. He stiffens. "Cruz. Look at me."

He stays as still as a statue for a minute before reluctantly turning toward me. The console is the only thing between us.

Reaching out, I take his hand and trace the veins popping out with his tense stance. "Why is it complicated?"

He looks down and watches my fingers trace the length of his hand. Muttering so lightly I have to strain to hear him, he says, "It just is. There are things you don't know. Bad things. Things I don't want you to know."

My hand stills. *Bad things? Like what? What could be so bad that he's built this wall around himself? Was he abused? Molested? I don't understand what he's talking about, but I want him to share it with me. Nothing he can say is going to change anything I feel... right?*

"Like what, Cruz? You can talk to me. You should know that by now."

He nods. "I do know that. I know you say that, but I have a feeling it won't matter. It always ends up mattering to people. People think about me differently."

What on earth is he talking about? He's not making any sense.

"I have to admit, I'm lost here, Cruz. I know you have secrets. Hell, anyone can see that you have a wall up, but I really haven't the slightest idea as to why that is. I want nothing more than for you to talk to me. I'd be there for you. I would still be *here*. Nothing you can say will change anything about the way I feel for you, but you have to let me in.

"I can wait. I'm not pushing, but I want you to tell me, when you're comfortable. I just can't do this anymore. I want you. I care about you. I want things to move on to the next level with us, but you have to give me something. You have to either tell me that you want me too or you don't. I promise I'll be fine with either, but you have to give me at least that."

Shit, Tif, nothing like laying it all out there.

I know that breaks every rule, but shit… I need an answer and he's going to give me one.

Cruz is still just watching me, saying nothing. Finally he nods.

What the hell is the nod about? Does he think he just answered me? What the hell?

He puts the car in reverse and backs out. What the hell?!

I stare at his profile in confusion. What was the nod about? Was he saying he *is* interested? Is he saying he's not? That nod has me more confused than anything he's done up until now.

I watch Cruz expertly handle the sports car through traffic. He drives fast, but cautiously. Within ten minutes, he's pulling up at my small house. He pulls into the driveway and parks before he looks at me. The security light came on when he parked, so his face is illuminated. *God, he's perfect.*

We sit in silence and I pick at the seam on my jeans. He

doesn't talk, but then again, he's never been much of a talker. Eventually, I can't take it anymore. I blurt out, "What the hell was the nod for?"

He lightly chuckles. "I knew that would eat at you."

Slapping the seat in frustration, I lean back and glare at him. "Well yeah! What did it mean? You want me? You don't? I need more than a nod, Cruz!"

He leans over and gets into my space as he pulls the handle on my door. He gestures out. "Let's get out."

I'm going to kill him. Is he purposely trying to drive me batty? Every question is just ignored or he's evasive with his answers. Dammit man, throw me a breadcrumb!

I get out and stomp up my steps before throwing myself into the cypress swing hanging from the rafters and watch him.

Ok, maybe that was juvenile, but he's literally making me crazy!

He trails up the steps and leans casually against the post as he watches me with a slight smile.

"Are you enjoying pissing me off?" I throw out at him.

He can't help it, he laughs. The sound is so amazing, I can't stop the smile that spreads across my face or the heat that pools in my center.

Crossing the porch, he joins me on the swing and uses one foot to gently push us. He's on one end and I'm on the other. He laughs again. "I am enjoying your huffing and puffing."

I slap his shoulder and the muscles jump. "That is so rude."

He looks at me and his face sobers. We stare for a long time before he again turns away and looks through the trees and up at the moon. He speaks and I watch the shadows dance across his face. "Ok, Tifanie. I'll tell you a little something…"

Chapter Five

Cruz

*A*m I really going to do this? Am I really going to talk to Tifanie about my demons? Am I ready to open myself up to anyone?

I'm not actually, but she's been brutally honest with me. She deserves to know. At least a little bit.

Here goes nothing…

It's a beautiful night. It's not sweltering hot and there's actually a cool front, so with the breeze, it's about seventy out here. Tifanie's porch is nice. It suits her.

Nature relaxes me, so I watch the breeze through the leaves as I decide to tell her some of my past.

Her breath catches, almost as if she's startled I'm really

going to tell her. I can't really blame her. I'm a pretty secretive guy.

"My momma is amazing. She raised me on her own. She was right at twenty-one when I was born. She worked for an architecture firm in Baton Rouge. She was in college for architecture, so the internship was exactly what she wanted.

"The day she started at the firm, she met one of the partners. He was wealthy and a little older than her, but he seemed to like her. She was focused on getting through college and soaking up all the knowledge she could gather from working at the firm.

"He asked her out for drinks and dinner almost daily, but she always politely declined. Something about him made her uncomfortable, but she said she couldn't put her finger on what exactly. This went on for months.

"A large contract came to the firm and they had late nights and all hands on deck to perfect the proposal. The partner started flirting more and more with my momma as they worked closer and closer together.

"She continued to decline. The firm got the proposal and everyone went out to celebrate one night. It was at a bar and people were drunk. She left after a couple of drinks because she had class the next morning and while she unlocked her car, he followed her. He was drunk and aggressive. She declined his advances again and he lost it. He beat and raped her and then he freaked out and stole her purse to make it look like a robbery.

"He left her there… in the dirty parking lot of a bar while he went back in and had more drinks.

"She was able to identify him after she was examined and cleaned up in the hospital. He was arrested and eventually convicted, but he left a permanent reminder… me."

I watch Tifanie as I say the last part. I want to see her reaction. Her eyes widen, and her hand flies to her mouth, but she doesn't say anything.

I tell her the rest. "I'm the child of a rape, Tifanie. My momma is black. The man who raped her is white. I'm a mixed child resulting from a heinous act."

She swallows and looks at me. Her eyes are glassy, but she doesn't speak. Finally, she removes her hand and lets out a long, drawn-out sigh. "Cruz, I am so sorry for your mother. No woman should ever have to deal with that. I see it more than I ever want to." She looks at me and cocks her head to the side as she concentrates on my face. "I'm confused though. I knew you were mixed. You are in fact black, though you are light and your eyes are blue. Was that supposed to come as a shock to me?"

Does she really not understand? She's acting like I'm mixed is what she should be scandalized about. Did she not hear the part about me coming from a rape?!

I am in shock. "No, I know you know I'm mixed. I just told you I came from a rape, Tifanie."

She nods. "I know. I heard you. Every word. But what I'm confused about is why you think that has any bearing on you. You are a good man, Cruz. You are loyal and smart and beautiful and talented. Why do you think the sins of your father have anything whatsoever to do with you?"

Is she serious?

"What? How can you say that?

"The only reason I exist is because a man whose blood created me raped and beat my mother. His blood is in me, Tifanie. He's a part of me."

She shakes her head and takes my hands. "No, Cruz. You're wrong. Yes, he helped create you, but *you* define you.

"What I see is a man who is letting the shame of someone else's acts make him feel inferior. You are not. You are amazing. And your mother should be very proud of this amazing man you are. She molded you. You learned from *her* not from him. I don't believe that he's a part of you. I believe that we define ourselves."

Does she mean that?

I swallow as my chest gets tight. The guys have said as much for years now, but they know the story. They know everything. Can Tifanie really be serious?

My hands cradle hers and I tighten my fingers. "What?"

She smiles and leans over, closing the distance between

us. She looks into my face and squeezes my hands. "Cruz, I wish you could see what I see…"

Without thinking it through, I close the remaining distance and capture her mouth. She gasps as she's taken by surprise. Her hands leave my hands and trail up my arms before circling my neck. Her head angles, giving me better access. She moans into my mouth as she opens her lips to grant me the access I've been craving.

I didn't realize how badly I've wanted the feel of her mouth on mine. Our tongues weave a magical spell as they dance.

She moans my name as she breaks the kiss, only to climb across my lap and straddle me on the swing before meshing her mouth once again to mine.

My hands are weaving through her hair, anchoring her head at the angle that I want it. She runs her hands over my shoulders and down my chest and abs before running them back up. She's tracing all of the ridges.

She moves again and we almost fall off the swing. It interrupts us and she breaks the kiss to keep from falling backwards.

Leaning her head into my neck, she breathes deeply. I lay my head back and try to gather my thoughts. That was... incredible.

A chuckle against my neck makes me smile as she mutters, "Um, ok then. You are a mighty fine kisser, Mr. Edwards."

I laugh as I pull back and look at her. Her cheeks are flushed and her eyes are sparkling. "You're no novice yourself."

She laughs again and stands up, holding her hand out to me. "I'm getting chilly since I'm not climbing you like a monkey on a banana tree anymore. Let's go in. I want coffee."

My eyes widen. She laughs even harder. "You can keep your clothes on. I'm not asking you to share my bed. Well, unless you want to uncover all those glorious muscles, in which case I will certainly not complain. You can certainly consume your coffee shirtless! I'm just saying let's go inside."

Feeling surprisingly lighter, I shake my head and chuckle again. "Ok."

I love that she's so confident and sure of herself and what she wants. It's refreshing without being obnoxious. She's so sexy without really trying. It's damn interesting and takes a lot of the pressure off of me.

She unlocks the door and turns on the lights as we enter. Walking to her kitchen, she calls over her shoulder, "Besides, you don't get any of this until you answer my question."

Answer her question?

I did that. Didn't I?!

No, you did not answer her. Because you still don't know if you're going to go for it. Yet, after that kiss, the thought of anyone else sampling Tifanie does not sit well with me. Not at all...

Hell no, that is not happening.

I decide to act out of character. No time like the present to make a stand. With my decision made, I head into the kitchen. She turns and once she sees the look in my eyes, she watches me warily as I cross over to her, take the coffee cup out of her hand, and place it on the counter.

She looks up at me. She's tall, but I'm taller. She swallows. "Um, what are you doing?"

I chuckle again as I back her into the counter. Leaning down, I talk softly against her lips, "Answering your question," and then gently brush my mouth against hers.

She shudders and whispers, "What was the question again?"

Laughing, I lean down to kiss her lightly before pulling back and staring into her hazel eyes. "The question of what I want."

She nods. "Ok, so what do you want?"

Leaning down and answering her as I look deep into her eyes, I say with the utmost sincerity, "I want *you*."

Leaning her forehead against mine, I can see her smile. "Thank you, Jesus. It's about time!"

I laugh and push down the fear. I just took a huge chance

on not just myself, but her too. Right now, I just want to relish it. I'll deal with the fear later.

Can I do this? What am I about to take on? Are we going to date? Is she going to see other dudes? Like Remy?

Hell no. No, she's not. No other dudes. Just me.

Me and Tifanie... I think we've crossed the friend barrier.

Hell, if you weren't a scaredy-cat, Cruz, you could have crossed it long before now.

Man, I'm going to get so much shit for this...

Tifanie snaps me out of my musings with a towel slap to my rear. "You want some coffee? I have Community Pumpkin Praline."

I nod. Coffee is good. "Sounds great. You have creamer, too?"

She laughs and points to the fridge. "I do. Pumpkin Spice and Vanilla Latte. Take your pick. Hand me the pumpkin, though."

I can't help but laugh as I open the fridge. She sees me

looking and shrugs and smirks. "What can I say? I'm a pumpkin whore!"

A pumpkin whore?!

I grab one of the bottles and close it as I turn. Holding it out, I ask, "Six bottles? Are you really going to drink all of that?"

She sticks her tongue out at me and takes the bottle, making sure to touch me. She watches me to see if I'm going to pull back from her, like I usually do. I don't. She smiles.

"Yes, I will drink all of it and probably buy more if it's still out. It's hard to find and it's my fave."

We chit chat about Halloween, which is next month, while the coffee brews. She's a big fan of the holiday and says whenever she's not working for it, she dresses up and goes out. She mentions that this year she's going to be Black Widow and she's scheduled to be off for the annual Baton Rouge Halloween Parade. My brows raise as I think about her body in that tight black costume. She smirks and coyly says, "Care to be Captain America and join me?" I laugh and shake my head. No way in hell I'm dressing up like Captain America for Halloween. "No to Captain America. Yes, I'll join you though." I smirk. "I'm more of a Director Fury man." I wink.

Once we get the coffee, we head into her living room and get comfy on the couch while she pulls up Netflix. She presses against me and I let her. I even move my arm, so she can lean against my side. It's new and unexpected, but it's like I just know what to do. Maybe it's just that I know what to do with Tifanie.

She asks if I want to watch Hocus Pocus and I laugh. "You really are in love with Halloween, huh?"

She nods. "I am. I love it. It's so fun and I go all out with the kids and stuff. Growing up, the annual Halloween party was one of the few things I really enjoyed with my family."

She never talks about her family, so my interest is piqued. But she doesn't say anything more and we settle in to watch the movie. Snuggled together on the couch under a blanket, drinking pumpkin coffee.

This is nice. Almost too nice…

Chapter Six

Tifanie

I stretch with a huge smile on my face as I start to awaken. Looking at the clock, I see it's after ten. I was exhausted after my twenty-four hour shift, the game, and then Cruz telling me his story. I knew there was something, but I wouldn't have guessed that. I knew he was mixed, but I assumed it was just a regular relationship. I had no idea about his mother being raped.

What an amazing woman she must be. To not only deal with the rape, but to keep, nurture, and love the child that came from it. She's a very strong woman and I hope one day to be blessed enough to meet her.

I see a lot of ugly with my job. We've been called to

rapes, beatings, shootings, and all sorts of other sordid things. To know that Cruz's mother endured that... I can't imagine.

I just hope that he understands his parentage has nothing to do with him and everything to do with the bad choices the man who fathered him made.

I'm going to make it my mission to break the rest of those walls down. Last night was a great start. He wants me! I knew he did. Well, I hoped he did, but I wasn't certain he'd admit it to himself.

He did though. He admitted it to himself and to me. That's progress. I am patient and stubborn. I can wear him down and wait him out. Because at the end of this, I want the prize. I want not just the man, but the man's love. And I intend to get it.

Right now though, I am off today and my plans are to go volunteer at the Food Bank. I dance around as I shower and get ready. One of my favorite songs comes on the radio and I can't help but shake my hips as I sing as loudly as I can all about my bass.

The song makes me laugh, but I love it and the beat. The message is great too.

Half an hour later, I throw my hair into a ponytail and grab my purse as I head out the door. I'm craving a Caramel Apple Latte and the only place in town to get one is Java and Sweeties. Of course the possibility of seeing Cruz never even crosses my mind.

Yeah, right.

I head out to my garage and back my SUV out and my phone rings. Glancing down, I see my sister's name. Hitting ignore, I throw my phone onto the seat. No idea what she wants, but whatever it is, I already know I'm not interested.

I sing while I navigate traffic. It's surprisingly light as I make my way through campus.

As I pull into the parking lot of Java and Sweeties, I look for a red sports car. It's not there and I push down my slight disappointment. I came here for the coffee, not the possibility of seeing a sexy, blue-eyed, caramel-skinned drummer.

I'm humming as I walk in and make my way to the counter. The place is packed with only a couple of empty spots in it. Glancing over toward the table that Bayou Stix and company usually frequents, I see my girlfriend Melonie, and her boyfriend Dade, Cruz's bandmate. They see me and wave. Mel motions me to head over by patting the seat next to her. I nod and approach the counter. Erik, the proprietor and another friend of Cruz's, is behind the counter. He smiles as he sees me. "Hey, Tifanie. What can I get you today?"

Smiling at him, I reply, "An extra-large Caramel Apple Latte with fat-free milk and whipped cream, please!"

He laughs. "You've got it. You want the sugar-free syrup too?"

Frowning, I say, "No way. Gross. I want the sugar."

He laughs as he calls my order out to the baristas. I can't help checking him out in his very well-fitting apron. He's gorgeous. He's built with chestnut hair and sparkling blue eyes. He looks up and catches me perusing him. He winks.

"Whatcha looking at?"

I smirk. "A fine assed man."

He feigns shock and looks around me. "Where? I still like to look!"

Slapping my money down, I chortle. "You, dumbass! You know you're fine. I love to look at you."

He bats his eyes and pushes my money back. "On the house, babe. Thank you. Head on over to the table. I'm taking a break in a bit and I'll bring your coffee."

Rolling my own eyes, I push the ten into the tip jar and stick my tongue out at him as he tries to stop me, before heading to the table.

I've hung out with him, his boyfriend, the band, and their women a bit over the past few months with Cruz, so I'm comfortable with everyone and I know Melonie very well. We're the same age and attend a lot of the same functions since she's a doctor and I work so much as a paramedic.

Mel smirks at me as I get to the table. "Hey, girl. Meeting Cruz?"

At the mention of his name, my heart races. I can't help it. It's just a natural reaction and it's been that way since the first time I saw him. What's funny is the first time I saw him was on a call at Dade's house. Dade wasn't there, but there was a 911 call and Ty and I responded. It was Clove, Dade's little sister, and I met Liam and Cruz. Clove was pregnant and had kidney stones. She's now married to Liam and due any day.

Shaking out of my memories, I smile back at her. "No. I'm off and thought I'd go volunteer at the Food Bank today, but I had a craving for a Caramel Apple Latte first."

She nods. "A latte, huh?" Smirking, she says, "I see. Well, he should be here any minute. He's supposed to go with Dade to get some new banisters for the house."

What the hell? He's on his way here?!

Why are you acting surprised? Isn't that why you came here, just hoping to see him?

Ugh, I'm so predictable. Is he going to think I'm a stalker?

Shut up! No, I'm not a stalker. I wanted a coffee. A coffee that is

delicious and they only make here. And ok, I might have wanted to see
Cruz, too.

Dammit, I'm so busted.

I nod. "Are y'all remodeling?"

Dade scratches his head. "No, not really. But there's one banister that the college kids just tore up. Even with all the sanding and refinishing I've done, it just looks bad since it's gouged pretty bad with large chunks missing. I just want to replace it. Cruz is going to help me muscle the wood." He winks and flexes.

My pulse quickens. *Dear lord... why are these men so attractive?*

I sigh and Mel mimics it and mutters, "I know, right?!"

Turning my head sharply, our eyes meet and we both laugh. She giggles and nods at the door. "Your boy is here. And he looks downright chipper today." She looks at me inquisitively. "You wouldn't know anything about that, would you?!"

I turn to watch Cruz approach. The fact that heads turn

as he passes, both male and female, is *not* lost on me. My stomach does flips. He sees me at the table and stops for a second. My heart drops, but then he smiles at me and the breath whooshes out of my chest. Thank God I'm sitting down because I'd collapse from the power of that smile. *Dear God!*

Erik arrives at the table at the same time with a tray of coffees. He passes them out and pulls out a chair. Cruz sees my monster-sized coffee and says, "Do we need a coffee intervention here?"

Taking a sip I let out a moan as it hits the back of my tongue. That is seriously like heaven. The coffee with the sweetness of the caramel and apple and then the creamy whipped cream… It should be illegal.

Cruz smirks slightly at my reaction, though his eyes are wide and I see him watch me swallow. I lick my lips and he follows the trail with his eyes. He asks, "I guess that's good?"

I nod and hold my cup out. "It's divine. Try it."

I'm daring him and I've forgotten that anyone else is even in the room. He stares at me and I see his light eyes darken as he covers my hand with his and guides the cup to his mouth. He takes a sip in the same spot as I just drank from.

Suddenly butterflies are dancing in my stomach and I feel like I just went over the drop on a rollercoaster. I gasp as I watch him swallow. He has a tiny bit of whipped cream on the side of his mouth and I just want to lick it off. He pops his lips and wipes the side of his mouth before sucking the tiny bit of whipped cream off. Staring into my eyes, he says, "Yes, that is definitely good. Thanks for letting me sample your treat, Tif."

My mouth hangs open and the only thing that wakes me from my trance is the light coughing behind me. Shaking my head, I turn and see Dade, Melonie, and Erik all staring at us with wonder on their faces. I have no idea who even just coughed.

Mel is looking from me to Cruz in glee and Dade is trying to hide a smirk. He says, "Well, I'll be damned…"

That wakes me up. I slump back onto my stool and glance at Melonie. She's looking at me with a face full of questions. I shake my head slightly to tell her, not right now.

She smiles and lets me know she understands, but I'm not off the hook.

Holy shit. I've thought Cruz was gorgeous from the very first second I saw him. I wanted him that night at the house, but as time went on and I saw him more and more, the feelings grew. Now, we've been friends for a few months and then last night we kissed… now I can't stop picturing him naked.

Snap out of it, Tif! You can't push him or you'll spook him. He'll bolt so fast you won't even have time to react. Calm your ass down!

Shit, I need a tub of ice and a fan.

While I've been trying *not* to fantasize about Cruz, I've missed the entire conversation at the table. I'm only brought back to reality as Erik stands up, saying he needs to get back to work and Cruz leans back to stretch while Dade kisses Melonie before he stands up too.

What did I miss?

Melonie is staring at me. Did she say something? Is she waiting for a response of some sort?

Everyone is staring at me and I have no idea why. *Son of a bitch...*

Cruz leans down and asks, "You ok with Mel hanging with you at the Food Bank while we go get the wood?"

Oh, so she did ask me a question.

I chuckle. "Of course." Breaking my gaze from Cruz, I look at a delighted Melonie. "The more the merrier. You're more than welcome to join me."

Cruz stares at me like he has something to say, but then he just smiles and heads off with Dade. As he reaches the door, he turns and calls out, "Hey, Tif. Call you later."

He waits for me to nod before it closes behind him.

I let out the breath I was holding as it closes.

Melonie laughs and says, "What the hell? What was that?"

Looking at her, I smirk. "Honestly, I have no idea."

She looks at me in disbelief. "He just sat here smiling for about twenty minutes, Tifanie. Cruz did! Like constantly. He doesn't do that. So, what are you not telling me? Did something finally happen?"

A soft voice behind me chimes in. "I want to know the answer to that too!"

Turning, I see Lexi, Jude's wife, and the owner of the bakery part of this amazing establishment, standing there. I can't help but let my gaze travel over her petite frame. She's gorgeous and curvaceous, but she's also got an adorable little baby bump now too. She pulls out one of the high-backed chairs and sits down while she picks her feet up onto another chair. Melonie nods approvingly.

Her hands rest on her little belly and she laughs. "Erik and Jude insist on me taking breaks every few hours. If I forget, Erik turns into a bossy bear, so here I am. And I caught the tail end of that interesting little scenario just now." She looks right at me. "So, do tell, Tifanie!"

Melonie joins in. "Good for the men folk. You need to

take frequent breaks." She turns to me. "Yes, you have four very eager ears. Enlighten us. You and Cruz. What happened?"

I feel my cheeks flush and I chuckle. "Nothing really." They both look at me, not buying it. I relent. "Ok, I told him what I wanted last night." They both lean forward. "And I kissed him."

Lexi says, "*You* kissed *him*?!"

Melonie butts in. "But, not for the first time? That was not the first kiss. No way. Right?"

Do they not know Cruz? Yes, for the very first time. It's laughable that they are so shocked. Do they think we've been screwing?

Nodding, I say, "Yes, for the very first time. We've been dancing on eggshells. For months. We've been friends and while we've hung out, he's never even touched me. He's avoided touching me." I shrug as they blink. "Last night, I had enough and I laid it all out. I told him exactly what I wanted from him and asked him what it was he wanted. I kissed him first though."

"And, what did he say?" Lexi asks.

I smile as I remember. "He kissed me. And then said he wanted me too." I frown as I realize that's all he said though. Other than saying he wants me, he didn't really say in what capacity. I'm really no more informed than I was yesterday other than him admitting he wanted me and some kissing.

Well, shit! Why is this so freaking complicated? What happened to I like you, you like me, we're attracted, let's just be together?! Why does it seem like the older you get, the harder relationships get? Shouldn't that be the opposite?!

Melonie is watching me. "What's that look for? What's wrong?"

Before I can answer, both of their cells buzz simultaneously. They look at each other in confusion and check the phones.

Lexi says, "It's time."

Melonie says, "I need to get to the hospital. Shit, I rode here with Dade!"

Erik calls out, "Y'all ready?" as he looks up from his

phone.

I look at them in confusion. Lexi says, "Clove just went into labor. Can you bring us to the hospital? None of us have a car right now. How fucking insane is that?"

Nodding, I hop up, grabbing my coffee and keys. "Yup. Let's go."

Erik tosses his apron under the counter as he calls out orders to the scrambling baristas, Lexi runs to grab her purse, and Melonie calls the hospital. As we head toward the hospital with Melonie getting stats, the excitement in the car is palpable.

Chapter Seven

Cruz

Oh boy. Liam just sent out a mass text saying Clove is in labor and that everyone can head to the hospital. Dade is freaking out, so I'm driving his Hummer. He's on the phone with Liam who is also freaking out because his wife is in labor. I can hear Clove in the background telling both of them to calm down and that women have babies every single day.

Of course she would be the calm one and she's also the one in labor.

It takes us about half an hour to get to the hospital and before I can park, Dade is out of the Hummer and sprinting through the doors. It makes me chuckle though I know everyone is nervous since Clove has had a rough few months. She's a little early, but the doctors, well, Melonie, says everything is fine at this point.

It's an exciting time. The first Bayou Stix baby. I'm happy for them.

My cell rings as I'm getting ready to get out of the truck. The number says, **"Unknown Caller."** How the hell is someone not in my Call List calling me? I have a private number. I don't answer it and let it go to voicemail.

It takes a few minutes since the caller is leaving a message. As soon as it pops up, I check it. As I listen, my fists ball and my eyes darken with rage. My head feels like it's going to explode. The message is long over but I can't get out of the vehicle. I'm so enraged, I'm scared to move. I'm lost in my own dark thoughts.

I don't even know how long I sit, but the ringing of my phone alerts me that it's been a while. Looking down, I see **"Dade"** on the display. Shaking my head to clear some of the rage, I take a deep breath and answer.

"Hey, man. Sorry, I'm on my way in now. Where am I going?"

"You ok? I've been in here almost an hour, Cruz. Melonie says she's doing well and with no complications. Baby John should be here shortly. Are you coming?"

I open the door and walk rapidly across the large parking lot. "Yes, I'm coming in now. I need to know where I'm going though."

Dade gives me directions and says Jessie and Blue are in the hall and will show me the way from the elevators once I get off.

I need to clear my head and not let the phone call mess with me. This is a happy time. I'm excited for my friends. No time to dwell on this bullshit right now. I'll deal with it later.

As I step off the elevator, I'm met by Jessie and Blue. Blue is talking animatedly and Jessie is just listening and smiling. I'm trying to listen to what she's saying, but I don't even understand half of it. It's like she's speaking Greek.

"Dilated nine centimeters… water broke in the kitchen… baby should be here really soon. Hoping the baby has dark hair…" I'm just staring at her as I try to take it all in. I don't know what any of that means.

Blue is leading us down a hall, chattering away. I look at Jessie and mutter, "What the hell does any of that mean?"

He shrugs and laughs. "I have no damn idea. I'm just nodding in agreement with her. I think it just means she's close and John will be here very soon."

We turn the corner and there's a huge crowd of people in the small hallway. Blue races over to Lexi and Bradi who are in the corner. Jessie and I head over to talk to Jude, Dade, Micah, Erik, Alec, and Mr. George. He's kind of Dade and Clove's surrogate father since they don't really have one. As we get there, Dade is on the phone and I catch the tail end. "Yes, sir. She's doing well. Y'all be careful crossing the Basin. Don't rush. Call back when you get here and we'll meet you downstairs. It's kind of a maze in here. Tell Ms. Verna to drive safely… See y'all in a little while."

He hangs up and looks at everyone. "That was Paw. Ms. Verna is driving them in. They should be here in another forty-five minutes or so."

I nod. "I'll go meet them when they get here so you don't have to leave."

Dade nods and claps my shoulder. "Thanks, man."

Liam pops his head out of the door and calls out, "Cruz here yet?"

I call out that I am.

He hollers, "Clove wants to see you. Come here."

I look at Dade in confusion and he shrugs. As I walk around him wondering what Clove needs to see me for right now, I see Tifanie step out from the group of girls. She sees the confusion on my face and mouths, "I brought Mel, Lexi, and Erik. No cars."

That's right. I knew they were all carless today. I smile at her in thanks and nod.

Liam hollers again, "Hurry up, dude!"

What the hell does she want? Is everything ok? Liam isn't

acting like something is wrong.

Walking into the room, I'm nervous. I don't like hospitals and I don't know why Clove wants to see me. She's grimacing on the bed when I walk in, like she's in pain. I frown and walk over. Melonie is in the room in scrubs and a white doctor's coat. She's monitoring a lot of machines and talking quietly to a nurse. She looks over her shoulder and smiles at me.

Walking to the bed, I take Clove's hand. "How are you doing, Clove?"

She chuckles and then grimaces. "I'm good, just in labor, which hurts like a bitch."

"You wanted to see me?" I'm perplexed.

She smiles at me and even with sweat and pain on her face, she's glowing. "I did. Can you call your mom? She's always been so sweet to me. I don't have a female around and, well, I wondered if she could come by if she has time."

Ah, of course. Clove and Dade's parents were junkies and left when she was just a baby. Dade raised her and she's never had a maternal figure. My momma always had a soft spot for her since we went to the same schools and are about the same age. I nod. "Of course. She'll love it. I'll go call her now."

Clove smirks at me. "I guess she'll get to meet Tifanie too, then."

Shit, I didn't think about that. But, yes, she will. Tifanie is here. Am I ok with her meeting my momma? That's kind of a major thing. But, it's Tifanie. If ever I was going to let any girl meet my momma, it would be her.

I'm just not sure I'm ready to answer the questions. I'm not certain I know how to answer them...

I realize I never answered Clove. "Yes, I suppose she will."

She smiles at me with a knowing look in her eyes. "Something is different."

"What do you mean?"

She points at me. "With you. Something is different. You look... lighter..."

I look lighter? What the hell does that mean? I looked heavy?!

I'm so confused by not only this conversation, but by the feelings and the complexity of the feelings running through me about Tifanie. "Lighter?"

She laughs and it ends in a groan as she grabs the bedpost and screams out. It only lasts a few seconds and then she breathes and cracks her eyes at me. "Sorry, contractions are a real bitch!" She looks over my shoulder and Liam pushes past me and takes her hand. She smiles at him before once again focusing on me. "Yes, lighter. Like you're not walking around with the weight of the world on your shoulders. What happened? You know you're going to tell me."

I chuckle. I better just tell her. She'll get it out of me anyway. "What do you mean what happened?" I'm stalling.

She glares at me. I'm taken aback. "You stop being coy, Robert Cruz Edwards! What is going on with you and Tifanie? She's here, you are visibly different. So, what happened? Are you a couple?"

Are we a couple?!

Um, no. No, we're not a couple. Are we?!

She frowns at the confusion on my face. "What's wrong? Tell me what that look is about."

Liam is fascinated by our conversation and just sitting on the edge of Clove's bed, rubbing her hand and watching us.

I shrug and scratch the back of my neck before massaging the sudden tenseness there. "I don't think we're a couple. I mean no. No, we're not a couple. But, I know we're not just friends anymore either."

She's rubbing her stomach and staring intently at my face. Her eyes are shifting and traveling over the planes before returning to my eyes. I hate when she does that. It makes me think she can see into my soul.

She finally smiles softly. "I see. She's busted through the gate."

The gate? What the hell is she talking about? I look at Liam in silent question.

He smirks.

Clove writhes again in pain before she looks at me with glassy eyes. "Sorry, Hun. I know this is uncomfortable for you. They're a lot closer together now. I meant that your heart is not locked behind the fortress you keep it in. Tifanie has forged through the gate."

My eyes widen. She chuckles. "I'm not saying you're in love, calm down. But, I am saying you care about her. And she's just what you need. You push and she pushes back. She's not going to walk away, Cruz. Figure it out. Take your time, but leave yourself open to the possibilities with her. Because I have a feeling that she's not going to allow you to run...And you need that..." She moans again and Liam looks at Melonie who is at the foot of the bed.

Melonie says, "Let's check and see how close you are because those contractions are on top of each other now."

Liam looks at me in fear and excitement. "We're about to have a baby! I'm about to be a daddy, man!"

I smile and get choked up at the emotion on everyone's

face as I head to the door. "We'll talk more later, Clove. Right now, you need to concentrate on having that baby. Good luck y'all."

Melonie is saying, "It's go time. Are you ready to push, Clove? With the next one, push when I say go, ok…"

I walk out. Clove's scream follows me into the hall and everyone stares at me. "She's pushing."

Dade jumps up and Mr. George grips his arm. "Calm down, son. Women have been having babies for thousands of years. Besides, Melonie is in there with her. No better hands for our girl to be in."

Dade's phone goes off and he answers, "Hello. Hey, Paw. She's pushing now… Yes… Ok, Cruz is going to come down to meet y'all and bring you up… Yes, sir… Ok, he's on the way down now."

He hangs up and I'm already on it. "Got it. Are they at the front entrance?"

Dade nods and stares at the door to the hospital room as it rattles with the sound of Clove's screams. We can also hear Liam talking to her through the door, but we can't hear what he's saying.

I turn toward the hall and Tifanie is standing there. She smiles at me and says, "I'll come with you, if that's ok."

I nod and gesture for her to go in front of me to the elevators. She smiles and steps around me, brushing against my arm as she does. I feel the charge all the way to my toes.

She pushes the button and we head down to the first floor. It's quiet in the elevator and we don't speak as the doors close. We stop a few floors down, but the hallway is empty, so we're still alone on the elevator. Finally, she turns to me and speaks. "You ok, Cruz?"

My gaze meets hers and we stare at each other in the elevator. I nod. "I'm good. Just a lot on my mind."

She clicks her tongue and bites the pink tip. "Like what?"

I shrug. "Just a lot of stuff."

She hums and stares at me. "Are you ok today about last night? Not that anything happened, but are you ok today?"

She thinks I'm freaked out about her?

Well, you are. Sort of. Yes, there's all kinds of shit going on in my head, but yes, some of it is her.

Leaning back against the wall, I cross my long legs and stare at her. "I'm good."

"You sure?"

I nod and stand up. She watches me. I take a step and am standing in front of her. Reaching down, I gently pull her and she comes forward. Her hands grip my forearms. Her head angles back and she looks up at me as I look down at her. Her hair is in a ponytail, and it's swishing from side to side, tickling my hands as they cup her sides. "Yes, I'm good," I say and then lean down to kiss her.

I wasn't even sure I was going to do that, but once she was staring at me and meeting my gaze with her wide hazel eyes, my head shut off and I stopped thinking so much. I just acted.

Her head angles as I hold onto her ponytail and deepen the kiss. She's pressed against the back wall of the elevator with my thigh between hers. The sexy moans escaping her throat are driving me on. I attack her mouth as if I'm consumed and the only thing keeping me sane is her lips on mine... her tongue dancing with mine. I can taste the lingering flavor of sweet caramel in her mouth.

We forget that we're in the hospital. I forget the enraging phone call and the fact that I'm meeting my friend's grandfather down here. I forget everything but the woman in my arms and the kiss that is rocking my world.

The ding of the doors doesn't even alert us to the fact that we've stopped.

An uncomfortable clearing of a throat is the only thing that breaks through the haze. Stepping back, I drop my hands and turn. A disapproving gaze is directed at me and a condescending glance is thrown my way. I stand taller and in front of Tifanie in a protective stance. I'm used to people looking at me like that, but I don't want it directed at her.

I open my mouth to apologize. "I'm sorr..."

But, the woman's shocked gasp and then, "Tifanie?!" cuts me short.

Looking at her, I can see the shock on her face as she looks around me at Tifanie. Then her disgusted gaze travels the length of my body before her accusing eyes center once again on Tifanie.

"Honestly, Tifanie. You can't bother to show up at events or even answer your phone, yet, here you are... consorting... with this *gentleman* in a hospital elevator. A *public* elevator?!"

Chapter Eight

Tifanie

I'm so involved in Cruz, in his toe-curling kiss, that I forget where we are. All I want to do is straddle him. I want him so badly my blood is like fire in my veins. He's occupied my thoughts, my fantasies, for months and I've wondered about his kiss. Now, I've experienced it and it's like nothing I could have ever imagined. It's far superior to anything I even dreamed of.

I can't help but wonder why he's such a fantastic kisser. How many women have tasted these perfect lips?

Actually, I don't want to know that. It's not my business, yet I know damn well I don't want anyone else to *ever* taste them again.

Nope, I want them. I want exclusivity and I want it now. I want to mark him, to brand him. I'm scaring myself with the depth of my feelings. Dear lord, it's just a kiss. But holy shit, what a kiss it is.

Cruz occupies every atom of my being. The feelings he invokes in me have me unaware and uncaring of our surroundings. He breaks the kiss and I feel him stiffen. It frustrates me. How dare anyone or anything disturb my euphoria? But then… I comprehend the tone of the disturbance.

Standing tall, I straighten my shirt where it's ridden up from Cruz's hands on my sides. Looking around him, I gasp. I take in the perfectly pressed, expensive Alexander McQueen suit, pointy-toed Christian Louboutin heels, pearls, and not a hair out of place coiffed blonde updo. I take in the wrinkled nose as if something foul smelling is in the elevator, before settling on the frosty hazel eyes of… my sister.

My back instantly straightens as I match her frosty gaze

with one of my own.

The next words out of her mouth infuriate me. "Honestly, Tifanie. You can't bother to show up at events or even answer your phone, yet, here you are... consorting... with this *gentleman* in a hospital elevator. A *public* elevator?!"

She speaks with disdain and it pisses me off. How dare she talk down to Cruz like that! She doesn't even know him.

Cruz is looking from me to AnnaBeth in confusion. He opens his mouth to say something again, but I throw my hand out and stop him from talking. "Excuse me, AnnaBeth. I'd say it's lovely to see you, but we both know I'd be lying and you know I pride myself on not doing that." Cruz stares at me with a frown on his face. "Yes, I got your calls. But since I didn't answer, one would deem that I wasn't interested in a conversation. At least most people would... after the first ten unanswered calls and unreturned messages."

She gasps as her eyes widen and she touches her pearls in feigned shock.

I roll my eyes and link my arm with Cruz's. "Yet, you

continue to call me. And, I continue to ignore you. As far as not showing up at events, I am busy. I have a life and a career and I'm not a puppet on a string, again, unlike *some people.* Furthermore, this *gentleman* you are so rudely labeling is a friend of mine. A *very good* friend and you'll do well to keep your judgments to yourself." I step up to her and drag Cruz with me. She steps back as we approach. "Now, excuse us. We have things to do." We step off the elevator.

She calls out just before the doors close. "Well, I'm sorry you're so ashamed of all of us puppets, but perhaps you can put that aside and at least show up to your grandmother's eighty-fifth birthday! It's this Saturday at Chateau du Bellaforte. That's why I've been calling you." The doors close behind her.

I lean back against the brick walls of the hospital and take a deep breath. My family gets my hackles up.

Opening my eyes, Cruz is staring at me with his arms crossed over his chest. His arms are bulging in his long sleeved t-shirt. They're so defined I'm mesmerized. Finally, I focus on his face and realize his eyes are narrowed on me and his lips are tight. He asks flatly, "Care to share what that was about and who exactly that was?"

I sigh and straighten from the wall. Here we go. "Not really, but I will. That was my sister... AnnaBeth... Bellaforte."

His mouth goes slack and his arms fall limply at his sides. "*Bellaforte?* Did you just say Bellaforte?!"

"I did. I'm a Bellaforte."

He takes a step back and when I try to walk toward him, he holds his hands out to ward me off. "Bellaforte? Like the political family Bellaforte? One of the richest families in the South?!"

My stomach drops. *Great. I knew this would happen.* I glare at him. "Yes, that one. My name is Tifanie Jeffries-Bellaforte. I don't use Bellaforte for obvious reasons."

He takes a few steps back and turns his back to me. What is he thinking? This is why I don't use my family name! I don't want the shit that comes with it. I'm not like them. I don't give a shit about money or titles. I only care about hard work and earning what you deserve. He keeps his back turned to me and I can see him taking deep breaths.

I walk over to him and touch his back. The muscles are so tight. He's as stiff as a board. "Cruz? Hey, I'm not like them. I don't use the name because I'm not like them. I'm still me. I'm just me."

He turns to me and his eyes are once again bleak. Whatever ground we'd gained, we just lost. His walls are back up.

He steps forward and my hand falls. He says, "We need to get Liam's grandfather. It's why we're here. We need to get them up there to see the baby."

I nod as my chest hurts. I hold it in and push it down. This is not the time to hash it out about who I am. Or who he thinks I am. I'm me. I'm the girl he knows. The girl he's spent time with over the past few months. He *knows* me. I just need to remind him of that. Who I am is not my name. Who I am is who I choose to be!

I look at the parking lot and see an older couple slowly

making their way to the entrance. I ask Cruz, "Is that them?"

He looks at me briefly and in his eyes I see a hint of something I can't explain, but he masks it before he looks to the parking lot. He nods "It is." And he jogs to meet them. I don't know what else to do, so I head into the parking lot too and meet them all.

Cruz introduces me. "This is Tifanie. She's a paramedic and a friend to everyone."

Wow, ok then. I'm a friend to everyone. Nothing personal at all there. Son of a bitch. I could kill AnnaBeth. She's such a fucking snob. I can't stand to be around them. It's why I'm NOT around them all. My grandmother is the only one I can stomach. I do feel bad that I might have missed the party but why couldn't AnnaBeth just send a damn invite like a normal person?

Oh, that's right, she's not a normal person. She's a fucking Bellaforte!

La-Di-Fucking-Da!

I shake myself out of my mood. These are Liam's grandparents and this is a happy occasion. I put it aside for now, but Cruz and I are talking about this. He's not going to just push me away because of something like this. It has no bearing on me and no bearing whatsoever on what's happening with us! He's not getting away over something I can't control.

Nope, not happening. You might be stubborn, Cruz Edwards, but I have you beat!

I'm the queen of stubborn!

Chapter Nine

Cruz

---

*W*hat the fuck?! *Tifanie is from the richest and most influential family in Louisiana?! Are you shitting me right now?*

I can't even deal with that. I can't deal with that on top of the bullshit with my felon sperm donor and the upcoming tour. Not to mention that we're at the hospital and two of my best friends, my family, are having their first baby. I'm not dealing with this shit.

I can't be involved with her. She's a Bellaforte. I'm the child of a black woman and a white rapist. No, any illusion about Tifanie and me was just firmly shattered. People like her don't get involved with people like me. It doesn't happen. It can't happen.

It's not happening.

Thankfully, Paw and Ms. Verna showing up allow me to leave the conversation with Tifanie. I run across the parking lot to meet them and leave her in the entrance to the hospital. Maybe it was shitty, but I can't handle all this right now.

I see her face when I introduce her to Paw and Ms. Verna. It falls and the hurt is visible before she hides it and smiles at the older couple. "Hi. I'm Tifanie. It's nice to meet you. We just came down and things are progressing rapidly up there. I think Baby John will be here very soon."

Paw looks at Tifanie and as he takes in her appearance, he smiles. "Hello, Miss Tifanie. Aren't you a pretty thing?! Did you know that John was Liam's brother's name?"

I can see the wheels in her head spinning, but she smiles and says, "Thank you, sir. I did not know that. But, that's awesome."

Paw looks at me and then at Tifanie. "It is. John is here with us today and that baby has one hell of a Guardian Angel."

I can see the confusion on Tifanie's face. I decide to enlighten her. "John was a soldier. He was killed in action in Afghanistan years ago."

She gasps. "Oh my. I'm so sorry. I—I didn't know."

Paw pats her hands. "Walk with me, pretty girl." Tifanie takes his hand and they walk ahead with him telling her stories about John. I hear Paw say, "It's alright. God knows what he's doing. We don't always understand the why when it happens, but eventually it makes sense to us. John was a good boy. A good man. He's left quite a legacy."

His words send a pang to my heart.

Before I can dwell on them, Verna takes my arm. "Walk an old lady up? Nothing like having a good looking man on your arm to make everyone jealous." She winks at me.

I chuckle lightly. "Yes, Ma'am. Of course. How are you, Ms. Verna? How was traffic on the Basin?"

She tells me about their trip and how excited they are to see the baby, Liam, and Clove. Tifanie has held the elevator for us and we all pile on. As the two elderly people talk back and forth and bicker, I look at Tifanie across their heads. She's looking at me and she looks sad. I rapidly look away and I think I hear her sigh.

I'm sorry, but it has to be done. I'm no good for her. She's better off with someone in her own class. Someone more... like her.

I can't think about all of the "what could have beens."

It's just after 4PM when Liam pops his head into the hall and says, "He's here! John Zachariah Christianson is here! Seven pounds, seven ounces, and seventeen inches long! He's gorgeous! He looks just like his momma, but he has blue eyes!"

We all cheer and cat-call our congratulations as he mutters that he needs to get back in, but he'll be back out with photos shortly. He also says that in a few minutes they'll let people in to see Clove and the baby after they clean him up and get her situated.

We're all so elated. Blue and Lexi say they are running to the Gift Shop and tear off toward the elevators with Bradi and Erik hot on their heels. All the other guys high-five and Dade passes out cigars he bought just for the occasion.

Looking around, I see Tifanie off by herself, leaning against a wall. I watch her while she stares at the floor and come to a decision. I cross the hall. As I approach, her head rises and she looks at me. It's been a long day and some of her hair has escaped her ponytail, so wisps are here and there. She looks gorgeous. I tamp that back and stand next to her, propping my foot against the wall.

She turns her head. "So, a healthy baby boy. That's great. I'm happy for them."

I smile. "Yeah, they'll be amazing parents. I'm proud of them both."

She nods and taps her fingers on her pants legs before she straightens. "I'm going to head out. I know this is private and I don't really fit in here."

I know I should stop her, but I can't. I think it's best that she goes.

She pauses like she expects me to stop her, and then she smiles sadly. "I'm also going to give you some space. I know that my name is a big deal... to you." I stare at her. "It's not to me. I don't use it. I don't. I'm not a Bellaforte, Cruz. I'm Tifanie Jeffries. I'm the same girl I've been. I still want what I want. And that's you." My mouth pops open. She holds her hand out to silence me. "No, you don't talk right now. I'm leaving. I'm going to go home and drink some wine. Or Fireball, I could probably use the whiskey. But I'm not staying away. You and me... that's something real. We have something and my name doesn't change that. You know me." She reaches out and touches my face. I let her. "You know *me*. Whatever is going on," she taps my forehead, "in here. I'm going to give you a night to stew on it. But tomorrow, tomorrow I'm coming back... guns blazing. I'm not walking away. You're not pushing me away." She leans up and gently brushes her mouth against mine before stepping back. "I'm going to fight for you, Cruz Edwards." I can't speak. I just stare at her. She smiles at me. "Be ready."

She turns on her heel and walks away, leaving me in a stupor in the hallway of the hospital, surrounded by my friends, my family... the only other people who have ever fought for me...

Jessie brings me back to reality. He speaks from behind me. "Damn, man! That girl is dangerous!"

Turning, I look at him and he sees the look of utter bewilderment on my face. He laughs out loud and I see Jude and Dade high five. Jessie grins. "You're going down in flames, dude!"

Shaking my head, I flip them off and walk away. I hear them laughing behind me. I need to make a phone call. I promised Clove I'd call my momma. I need the distraction of talking to her and telling her about the baby anyway. I can't even let myself think about what Tifanie just said to me.

Dade calls after me, "Where you going, man? You're not leaving, are you?"

I wave at him. "No, I'm going to call my momma. Clove wants me to tell her about the baby and ask her to come visit."

He nods and says, "Ok, make sure you come back. They're going to want to see you."

I reply, "I wouldn't just leave, Dade. Just going to go out front to call Momma. I'll be back."

I call my momma and, as I expected, she's extremely excited to hear that Clove had the baby. She tells me that she's grabbing all the gifts she bought and she'll be on her way. Now why am I not surprised she bought a lot of gifts?!

I hang up after telling her to call me when she gets here so I can help her lug up all her stuff and she says she will. I need to head back inside, but I want a minute to breathe, so I find a bench and sit down. There's a really nice lake with a fountain and ducks out front, so I just watch it and allow my mind to clear.

I guess I was spaced out for a few minutes, because I never even heard anyone approach me, but a body plops down next to me on the bench. Looking over, I see Jude. He stretches his long legs out and leans back as he looks at the water. "Hey, man. Everything cool?"

I stare at a family of ducks in the water. It's a momma duck and five little ducklings. They are furiously splashing in the water. It looks like she's teaching them to dive. I watch them for a bit before I answer Jude. "Yes and no."

He looks at me. I stare ahead, just watching the ducks, but I see him incline his head as he watches me. "You know you can talk to me. You also know I won't push, but I'm going to give you some unsolicited advice." I look at him before looking back at the water. "I don't know what's going on with your birth father…"

I interrupt him. "Sperm donor. Not my father. Not in any aspect…"

I see him nod from the corner of my eye. "Ok, your sperm donor. I don't know what's going on. I know he's out of prison. I know he's contacted you." I look at him and swallow. "I know what he did to Corrin. That's all I know. I don't get in your business, man. But, I am here if you need me. You know that.

"I also know that something is up with you and Tifanie." I grip my jeans. "I don't know what's happening there either, but, I saw you today. You were looking at her. She was looking at you. Neither of you were looking when the other was. Then, you headed down here to get Paw and you both came back tense. You made it a point *not* to look at her. I heard what she said…" He looks at me again. "Cruz, she's a Bellaforte…"

I nod. "She is."

He shrugs. "So what?!"

I look at him incredulously. "So what?! So, she's a member of a political family. A major one. She's filthy rich. I'm a bastard and the son of a rapist. She's white blue-blood and I'm mixed! Her sister looked at me like I was the mud on the bottom of her five-thousand-dollar heels!" I shake my head. "We don't mesh. We don't belong. I'm bad for her."

He sits up quickly. His face is red and I can see the veins

in his head popping out. "Do you hear yourself? So fucking what? Yes, Tifanie is white. You're mixed, but, I don't see Tifanie dwelling on that! No, I see *you* dwelling on that. We, the band, we're your friends. We're your family. We care about *you*! And none of us give a shit about where you come from. So, some ignorant people give you shit about your skin color? So what? Fuck them! They don't *matter*, Cruz! The only people who matter are the ones who care and we do. Tifanie *does*!

"Yes, it sucks what happened to your mother. It fucking sucks and the fact that any man would do that to a woman makes me sick, but *that... that has nothing to do with you!* Yes, it's why you exist, but that act, that evil... that is not *you*. *That's him!*

"I don't want to see you push away the one person who is strong enough to put up with you and help you tackle your demons because you're scared she's too good for you. That is *her* choice, Cruz!"

I'm staring at him in awe. That was a pretty impassioned

speech.

He sighs and stands up. "Come back inside. Liam sent me to find you. Clove wants to see you." I stand too. "I'm sorry I came at you so hard." He bumps me with his shoulder. "I just care, man. We all do. I don't want you to go through what I went through. I lost Lexi for *seven years*, Cruz. Because I was stupid. Because we both were. I don't want that for you. You have a chance at something pretty fucking amazing here... Tifanie is good for you. She's what you need. She's what you deserve. Don't miss out on that because of something that has no relevence."

I don't answer him. I just clap him on the shoulder and we walk back into the hospital side by side.

The thoughts racing through my head now are ten times worse than they were when I first headed outside. Instead of things getting clearer about Tifanie, they just seem to be getting more and more confusing!

Chapter Ten

Tifanie

"Yo, Tif. Where are you, girl?" Ty calls out to me as we sit in the trailer during a lull in calls for the day.

Looking over at him sprawled out on the couch, I roll my eyes. "Sorry, what?"

He chuckles and sits up. He stretches and his back pops. "Where are you? You've been staring into space for the past half hour."

I pull my legs up and tuck them under me in the recliner as I focus on him. "I'm sorry. I didn't sleep that much last night. Some stuff happened with Cruz the other night and then things got weird yesterday. He backed off some, but I told him I wasn't going to let him run." I shrug. "I don't know where we stand… again."

Ty rubs his sage eyes and leans up on his knees as he observes me. "What do you mean? Tell me what happened and I'll try to decode for you."

I laugh. I know he's trying to help, but I can't get into it without sharing very personal stuff about Cruz and I just don't know if I want to divulge info that is not mine to share. Even with Ty. I kind of feel like that would be crossing a line.

Reaching over and snagging a few pretzels from his bowl, I crunch one as I think about what I can actually tell him. "Ok, well you know he's got some stuff going on. Well, I know about it now and it's a big deal. I'm not going to tell you what, because that's not my place, but it's a big deal."

Ty roughly asks, "Is he married?"

I chuckle. "What? Married?! Um, no. He's not married. He's actually single. It's nothing like that."

He frowns and cradles the back of his head as he leans

back and looks at me. "Well, ok good. Fill me in on what you can then."

"Well, long story short is he thinks I'm too good for him. He knows my name…"

That gets Ty's undivided attention. "Your name? You told him?"

I shake my head emphatically. "Nope. I did not. I would have. I was going to, eventually, but not now. People flip when they find out and I don't use it. You know that. I don't even mess with that money. I support myself!"

He nods in agreement. "I know you do. You bust your ass for everything you have. Your accomplishments are all your own Tif. Anyone who knows you, knows that!

"But, if you didn't tell him, then how did he find out?!"

I roll my eyes. "AnnaBeth!"

Ty coughs. "Your sister, hoity-toity, AnnaBeth?"

I chuckle at his description, but it fits. AnnaBeth is indeed hoity-toity. She's picture perfect. A mindless sheep who cares more about breeding and social standing than anything.

If you don't have large sums of money in the bank and the name to back it, you are nothing to her... and the rest of my family. I'm nothing like her... like any of them.

"Yeah, my sister. I was at the hospital with Cruz yesterday. Clove, you know the pregnant girl with the kidney stones call we went on a few months back?! She's married to Cruz's bandmate and her brother is dating Melonie." He looks confused. "Dr. Bird."

He nods in recognition. "Oh, sexy Dr. Melonie Bird and the call that changed your life and got you hooked on Drummer Boy?!"

I throw a pillow at Ty and he catches it and puts it behind his head. He winks at me. "You're not fast enough."

"Shut up! And yes, that call. Anyway, she went into labor and I happened to be at Java and Sweeties."

He mutters, "Nice coincidence."

I ignore him and continue. "Melonie was there when I arrived. Dade dropped her off and was going to pick her back up after running an errand. Lexi and Erik were also there... working. None of them had vehicles. I brought them to the hospital."

"All those rich people were there and none of them had a ride?!" He can't believe it.

"Yes, I don't know why. I didn't ask. But, I brought them to the hospital and then hung out for a bit. I went down to grab some of the family with Cruz and, well, we were hot and heavy in the elevator."

Ty whistles and grins wolfishly.

"Shut it. What are you, like twelve?! We were into it and missed the doors opening. AnnaBeth was there and disgusted with the PDA. Then she saw it was me... and well, that was fun."

Ty busts out laughing. "Wait?! You were all over Drummer Boy in the elevator and your snobby ass sister caught you? Red-handed? That is fucking priceless. Damn, I wish I'd seen her face!"

I can't help it. I chuckle. Her face was indeed priceless. Wish someone would have been there to snap a photo. "She looked like a fish out of water!" But, then I remember the look she gave Cruz. It makes my blood boil. "She was looking down on him before she ever saw me. She was judging him."

Ty sits up. "Some people are old-fashioned, Tif. You know that. Not everyone is up to date with the twenty-first century."

I nod. "I know. But the fact that she's my sister and we came from the same place just pisses me off. I don't think like that. I've never thought like that. My parents don't either. Not really. They are snobby as hell, but they aren't racist. They don't give a shit if someone is white or black. They only care about the name and what their bank account says."

Ty clucks his tongue. "Are you sure that's the way she was looking at him, Tif? AnnaBeth is snooty as shit. That's a fact, but I've never known her to look down at people for, well, race."

I look at him and raise my brow. "Oh, you spend a lot of

time with her?"

He visibly shudders. "Dear God, no. The thought of being around your Ice Queen sister for even five minutes makes my blood freeze and my dick shrivel. No offense."

I laugh. Sadly, I get it. "None taken. She's not a very warm person for sure. I get it. I don't care to be around her, at all. My parents either…"

That reminds me. Shit, my grandma's birthday is tomorrow. I love my grandma. Of all of my family, I'm very much like her. My parents are embarrassed by her because she is stubborn and headstrong and she doesn't give a rat's ass about money or social standing. She never has. She speaks her mind and is as blunt as the day is long. I love that woman.

My parents tolerate her because they have to. She's the bank. Well, the money is mostly hers. They can't bite the hand that feeds them.

Ugh, I need to go tomorrow. I just don't want to see my parents… or sister. Or whatever man they will throw at me because they think he's *suitable* and it's past time for me to stop this ridiculousness and marry into more money and produce perfect babies. I shudder.

"Hey, Ty?"

I can see he knows something is up. He cautiously says, "Yeah?" I give him my flirtatious smile and his back straightens. "What do you want? I don't like when you direct that smile at me. I usually don't like what follows!"

I laugh. He's right. We've worked together so long, he can read me like a book. "Well, it's my grandma's birthday tomorrow. Do you have plans?"

He throws a pretzel at me and glares. "Seriously? It's my day off and now you want me to spend it around your rude ass prissy family?!"

I mock glare. "Hey, you like my grandma!"

He chuckles. "I do like her. Mrs. Clarabelle Bellaforte is a gem! I love that woman. She's so spunky and always calling people out. She's awesome. It's the rest of them I can't stomach."

Batting my eyes at him, I smirk. "Please, Ty. You'd be doing me a huge favor. I can't go alone. They'll circle me and pounce. If you're there, I can have an excuse to ignore whomever they push me at. I'm certain he'll be perfectly pressed and cringe worthy! The 'perfect candidate' for a Bellaforte bride."

I can see he's going to agree. He frowns, but his eyes are twinkling. "Yes, we can't have that. Can I say something crass to AnnaBeth? And can I drink?"

I laugh. "Absolutely on both counts. I'll need a drink of my own!"

We are laughing at the likely scenarios for tomorrow when a call comes in. Time to get to work.

It's late. We've been here since 6AM and it's now a quarter after four. Only a little more than an hour left this go round and I'm exhausted. There are always more calls on the weekend, but with the weather changing and it not mimicking the temperature of Hell outside the past few days, people have been out and about a lot more and the calls are abundant.

I'm lying on the couch in the trailer and praying no more calls come in today. It's been quiet for the past hour though, so I'm scared to say anything and jinx it.

With the quiet, my mind is in overdrive and I can't stop thinking about Cruz. I know he thinks he's not good enough for me, but I also know he's wrong. I can't imagine what he's dealt with his whole life with his mom being raped and his dad being the wealthy white man who committed the crime. One thing I've learned in this line of work though is that evil is evil and it doesn't discriminate based on race, social standing, or anything else.

I bet Cruz has faced a lot of adversity because of his skin color throughout his life. I've witnessed it firsthand with some people. I've just never thought that way myself. I don't see a sexy black man when I look at Cruz. I just see a gorgeous man who interests me. I've never been interested in anyone like him before. Not because of his skin, but because of him. He's a rocker, but he's not anything like I'd imagine a rock star would be. None of the band members are. I've gotten to know them some over the past few months and none are what I would have imagined "famous rock stars" would act like. They are just regular guys. Gorgeous, regular guys who dote on the women in their lives.

I want to talk to him. I have a feeling he will avoid my call, so I'm going to do something out of character. Maybe it'll intrigue him enough to respond.

Taking out my cell phone, I type out a quick message.

"Tifanie:

I have something for you. Can I come by when I leave here tonight? Will you be home?"

Before I can overthink it, I hit send.

Letting out the breath I didn't know I was holding, I lean back with a throaty sigh.

Ty startles me as he laughs. I look up and he's watching me. "You send something to Cruz?"

I nod. "I did. I'm waiting to see if he's going to text back."

He laughs. "What did you send?"

I smirk. "None of your business."

He laughs and crosses over to the couch and plops down next to me. He swipes my phone out of my hand before I can react. "H-eeeeee-y!"

He laughs again and tries to open the app. "Was it dirty?"

Slapping his shoulder, I wrestle the phone away from him and laugh. "That is none of your business! And if it is dirty, you sure as shit don't need to be seeing it!"

Throwing his hands up in surrender, he laughs. "Hey, I can appreciate your hot bod. But no worries, I do not want to get intimate with you. Ewwwww."

I bust out laughing. "Thank God! Likewise!"

That thought makes me a little bit nauseated. That is one line we have never crossed. It's not one either of us is interested in crossing. It's refreshing to have such an amazing friendship without the drama of sexual attraction. Leaning back against the couch, I stare at the ceiling and watch the fan blades turn. Ty copies me. I see his head turn toward me from the corner of my eye.

Turning, I look at him. He has a serious look on his face. "Tif. Be careful. I know you want Cruz, but you said he stepped back. Again. I really don't want you to get hurt."

Sighing, I smile at him. "I know. I don't want me to get hurt either. I love you, you know that. You're the best. But, he's worth it." Turning, I stare back at the ceiling. "I just wish he realized that, too."

Ty claps my hand and squeezes. "Well, make him. If you really think he's worth it. Beat his ass down. Time to break out the big guns. Go big or go home, right?!"

Chuckling, I say, "That's the plan. This volcano is ready to erupt."

My phone buzzes just then. My heart accelerates as I lift the phone.

"Cruz:

I'll be here."

That's all he writes, but at least he responded. Time to kick this up a notch.

I want Cruz Edwards and it's time he realized I'm not backing down. He wants to run, that's fine, but I'm good at the chase and I have strong endurance.

I'm just not sure how to help someone overcome... himself.

Chapter Eleven

Cruz

Tifanie's text came through about half an hour ago. *She has something to give me? What does that mean? What could she have for me?*

I knew she'd call. She warned me. And she always follows through. Her word is as good as law. I've been thinking about it… about her… all damn day. Last night, too, if I'm being honest.

After talking to Jude last night, and then my momma, I know I can't keep pushing people away from me. More importantly, I can't push Tifanie away. Especially since she's the first woman in my life that I can ever remember wanting to hold on to. That scares the shit out of me.

After we left the hospital last night, I headed back to Momma's. She'd cooked dinner and wanted to talk. I didn't have much of a choice since Clove asked where Tifanie was, in front of her, at the hospital. I had to explain that Tifanie had been there but she'd left. Both women wanted to know why. That was a fun explanation.

Both got on my case and I listened. I didn't really have a choice, but then Momma wanted me to follow her home after Clove fell asleep. As we ate, Momma told me that she thought people were placed in our lives for a reason. She said that we all have a path and that everything that happens to us, good and bad, is part of a bigger plan. She's a woman of strong faith. It amazes me. She amazes me. After all of the horror she endured, her faith is unwavering. I want to get to that point. I want to be able to embrace what life has to offer; I'm just not certain how to do that.

I've pushed most people away for as long as I can re-member. I don't have the slightest idea how to take a chance and let someone in. My circle is extremely small and extremely tight.

You want Tifanie. I want Tifanie. I tried to deny it. I tried to push her away. I tried to get her to understand that we don't fit, but she's stubborn. She's determined and beautiful. She's exactly what I always imagined my woman would be. Well, if I ever thought I'd have a woman, which I didn't. Is Tifanie going to be that woman?

I can't stop thinking about her and I have a lot of excess energy, so I head out back to my gym. I had the old garage in my backyard converted about a year ago. I spend a lot of time in here so I didn't cut any corners. My gym easily rivals any of the membership gyms around. And it's mine. I can work out whenever I want to and be alone while I do it. It suits me.

As I turn on the music and let the beat start to pulsate through me, I can't stop thinking about Tifanie. Why is she coming over here? Not that she's never been here before. She has. More than once. We've hung out a good bit these past few months. Here, at her house, at Java and Sweeties… we've spent time together and with other people, but not a whole lot of time just the two of us. I always came up with a reason as to why that didn't need to happen.

Thinking back, I pushed and pushed her, but she stuck around. She's been a constant in my life for almost ten weeks now and I never even realized it. She's slowly but surely woven her way into my life. She's anchored her way into my thoughts… into my head… and my heart.

Son of a bitch.

Shit, I care about her. I really care about her. I've pushed my own feelings down or dismissed them as nothing for months now, but now I know. I know I care and she says she wants me. I told her I wanted her. She says she's not going anywhere. She hasn't, either. Maybe she really is here to stay.

Do I want her to stay?

She deserves a chance. Do I deserve the same chance?

Everything going on in my head is making me insane. It's information overload. I push my body so hard I'm surprised I don't crumple into a heap on the ground. At the end of my workout, I'm gasping for air as my chest rapidly rises and falls. Sweat is pouring down my face and chest and my muscles are burning.

Looking at the time, I see it's about the time for Tifanie to arrive. Doing a quick cool down, I wipe myself off with my shirt, and flip off the music and lights before locking the door behind me.

Heading back toward the house, I hear a car turn into my driveway. I decide to wait instead of going in. She'll be here in thirty seconds anyway. Her car rounds the curve and she parks under the basketball goal. We're staring at each other through the windshield. She smiles and my stomach drops.

I smile back and hers widens. She opens the door and steps out. All I see are bare legs. Miles of bare legs. What the hell is she wearing?!

I don't even realize I'm staring until she laughs. It's musical and seems to dance on the breeze. I hear her, but I can't look up from the very short skirt of her dress. Why is she wearing a dress?!

Her amused voice finally gets my attention. "I guess you

like my dress, Cruz?"

I swallow and look up from her legs. My gaze travels the path from her hips and torso before running over her bosom and resting on her face. She's smirking, but her gaze is devouring me. All I'm wearing are my trainers and red mesh shorts, which are low on my hips. She's fixated on my stomach. Looking down, I can't help but smirk as well. I guess she likes my hard work.

I am ripped. There's no other word for it. I work out every single day for at least two hours. I'm very defined and have lots of muscle without being a "meathead". My abs are streamlined.

That's where Tif's gaze is focused. She swallows. I suddenly feel a little flirtatious. Standing with my legs apart, I cross my arms and I don't miss the way her breathing accelerates as she notices all of the muscle on display.

Smiling at her response to me, I ask casually, "You want to come in? I need to shower."

She blinks, but doesn't look up at my face.

I chuckle lightly. "Tifanie." She finally raises her gaze. I point at the back door. "Do you want to come in? I need to go shower right quick."

She nods and I swear she mutters, "Jesus… the visual…"

It makes me feel amazing and I gesture for her to precede me. "Ladies first."

Her ass is cupped lovingly in the short black material and I watch it as she walks in front of me. I have the urge to touch and since I have no idea what is happening to me, I clench my hands at my sides, and stare at the sway of her hips.

She stops on the steps and her toned ass is in my direct line of sight. I hear a snicker and look up. She's laughing at me with mirth and desire in her eyes. "Are you checking out my ass?"

Busted. What can I do?!

Smiling sheepishly and shrugging, I say, "Sorry, busted."

Then, she surprises me as she shakes it in my face and says, "That's ok. I like it." She winks. "That's why I wore it."

And she walks into my house.

Dear lord, what is going on? I feel like I just jumped out of a plane and I'm not certain if the parachute will open.

I'm not sure what exactly is happening or why she's here, but I have a feeling shit is about to get real interesting.

Shaking my head and feeling an acute case of optimism, I take a minute to calm my thoughts and follow her into my house.

She's not in the kitchen, so I head into the living room. She's walking around looking at everything, trailing her fingers over the back of the couch. It's pretty sexy.

As she hears me, she turns and smiles at me. "Go ahead and get cleaned up. I'll just make myself..." she rounds the couch and sits and her skirt rides up to her crotch. It's barely covered. My mouth goes dry. "Comfortable."

I nod. The ability to speak alludes me. She chuckles as I head down the hall.

After flipping the shower on, I strip down and look at myself in the floor-length mirror, trying to see what Tifanie sees. I can't. I only see myself. Caramel skin over tight muscle, crystal blue eyes, full lips, tattoos on my shoulders and arms… I'm tall, over six foot, but I just look like me. I don't get the fascination. That's not to say I don't know I'm attractive. I do. I've heard it my whole life, but it was usually in the context of, "I can't believe he's so attractive."

Ugh. I don't have time for this. Shaking my head to stop the downward spiral, I step into the shower and quickly wash off. Within minutes, I'm done. Grabbing a towel, I quickly blot my skin and wrap it around my waist.

Shit, I don't have any clothes in here. I have to cross the hall. Tifanie is in the living room though, so I can make it without her seeing me. I feel weird though.

It's not a big deal. Grab some clothes to throw on and then let's go see what she has for me.

Opening the door, the steam billows into the hallway. I step out. The air is much cooler out here, so I stop for a minute to feel the difference on my skin. A gasp makes me jump and my towel loosens. Instincts kick in and I grab it before it falls completely off, but not quick enough to stop from flashing her.

I look up and Tifanie is staring at me and her mouth is opening and closing with no sound emerging. Her eyes are raking my body and though I have the towel on, I feel like I'm naked. My pulse quickens and the blatant appreciation and desire on her face has my groin stirring.

Shit! This is not good. Or is this very good?! I don't even know what I want right now.

I should walk into my bedroom, but I can't. I'm rooted to the floor with my anatomy lengthening as Tifanie rakes her gaze over me. It's almost like I can physically feel her gaze. It's like a caress.

Neither of us moves. She stares and I watch her… watch me. My hand is tightly gripping the cotton at my hip, keeping it covering the parts of me that are now standing at attention from the unadulterated lust on her face.

She licks her lips as she watches my cock lengthen and press against the towel. The gesture causes it to harden even more.

I can't breathe. I've had women before. A lot of them. I've had them want me, but I've never had anyone look at me like Tifanie is looking at me right now. It's so empowering.

The urge to take her, to claim her, to sear myself on her mind and body is suddenly too much to withstand. I can't stop myself. My hand loosens on the cotton and it falls. My cock stops its descent.

Tifanie watches with rapt attention and her bosom jerks with the deep breaths she's taking. Her legs appear to be shaking and she places her hand against the wall to steady herself.

With a little move to the side, the towel falls to the floor and I'm standing before her, fully nude in the hallway.

Her eyes drink me in and her hands are clenching and unclenching at her sides.

Nothing matters right now. Nothing except taking what she's willing to give. She told me she was here and she wanted me, she said her intentions were clear.

It's past time I took her up on her offer.

Chapter Twelve

Tifanie

---

*D*ear lord. Whatever picture I had in my head, whatever fantasy I conjured up, nothing compares to the sight in front of me right now.

Cruz is absolutely perfect. His body is pure perfection. The muscles are bulging and good lord, his dick is massive. I guess what they say about black men is true. I'm a little frightened, but I want him.

Is this really happening? I'm scared to move in case it's a dream and I wake up…

My gaze drinks in the magnificence of the man in front of me.

I'm in shape. I've been with men who cared about their bodies before, but never in my life have I witnessed such absolute perfection. It's almost like he's a painting on a canvas, an immortal god. I blink to make sure this is in fact really happening. Is he really standing in front of me like this?!

He's still there. Staring at me. I have to touch. I have to taste. I want to devour him. The air in the hallway feels electric.

Cruz is naked in front of me. I'm jumping at this chance. Taking a breath and standing as tall as I'm able on wobbly legs, I take a step toward him. He watches me.

Letting my eyes start at his feet, I travel his impressive height and memorize every plane and angle of his body. I want to remember this forever. As I get to his crystal blue eyes, I see pure want in them. His nostrils flare and he takes a step in my direction.

Two more from him has me pressed against the wall, his naked body against me. His cock is pressing against the apex of my thighs as he grabs my hair and tips my head back. Before I can breathe, he takes my mouth in a brutal kiss. It's hard and aggressive. One hand is holding my head back as he consumes my mouth. His tongue sweeps past my teeth as I gasp and he explores every recess of my mouth. My tongue immediately joins his. His other hand grabs my knee and curves my leg around his hip, pressing him more firmly against me. My short dress is pushed up and his hand palms my ass.

His lips leave my mouth and it feels bruised and swollen, but I don't care. The sensations are so exquisite I'm scared to move. I don't want to spook him and I'm praying he doesn't stop. His mouth trails over my neck and down to the scoop neck of my dress. His tongue trails across the tops of my breasts. I'm moaning and holding tightly to his head, keeping him in place.

His hands leave my hair and both cup my hips as his lips and tongue weave a sensual trail across my bust. I'm moaning and using the wall to hold myself upright on one leg as both hands cradle his head and hold him on my breasts.

His hands travel over my hips and push my dress up to

bunch at my waist. The cool air caresses my butt cheeks as they are exposed with only my tiny thong between us. His hands knead and caress my ass as his mouth finds a nipple through the dress. I'm dying here. "Ohhhh, Cruz. Touch me, please touch me."

He chuckles against my breast. "I am touching you."

Grabbing his head, I pull and make him look at me. His eyes are almost navy they are so dark with his arousal. Leaning in, I nip his full bottom lip and groan into his mouth, "No, *TOUCH ME!*"

Still staring into my eyes, he smiles and the beauty of it causes chills to race up my spine. His fingers push my thong to the side. The cool air teases my steaming folds. I bite my lip to stop from screaming out but a groan escapes from my throat anyway. His fingers brush across my mound. I push against his hand. He slips a finger into my wetness and I moan in appreciation. He mutters against my mouth, "Like this?" as his fingers enter and retreat at a leisurely pace. Throwing my head back, I thrust against his hand as he slowly and intimately fucks me with his fingers.

Opening my eyes, I can see the strain on his face. Bringing my head up, I wrap my arms around his shoulders and lean into his ear, taking the lobe into my mouth. He groans. I whisper, "Let go. Don't be gentle. I can take it."

His head snaps up and he grits his teeth. His finger picks up the pace. He adds a second one and then he's finger fucking me furiously. His fingers are ramming into me, and they're so long they are hitting my sweet spot. I'm wailing against the wall, my arms wrapped around his neck and shoulders are the only things holding me up. He rubs my clit with his thumb as he slams his fingers into me and his other hand grips my hip to hold me in place.

My eyes cross and I start shaking as the orgasm rolls through me. Screaming out, I shatter all over his hand. "Ohhhhh. Yes, baby. That's so good. *Finally!!* Dear God, *YES!*"

As I come down from my high, my leg slips off his hip. I open my eyes to glance at him and see the grimace on his face. Shuddering one last time, I stand with his help. "Why the grimace? Don't you dare say you regret that."

He chuckles. "No, I don't." He points down. "I'm just in pain here."

I laugh and give him a light shove. He looks startled. Stepping around him, I grab his hand and pull. It's soaking wet. "Come on, lover." Heading across the hall, I give his hand another yank. "I'm going to take care of that for you. It's your turn. I'm not nearly done with you." His brow arches. "My legs are jelly after that intense orgasm. I need a bed before I collapse."

He nods and follows me into his bedroom.

Taking a quick glance around, I notice the masculine colors, but, I really like the dark sleigh bed. It's about to get some use.

Cruz has allowed me to take the lead and I'm still extremely riled up, even after that amazing introduction in the hallway.

Turning, I grab him and move him in front of me. He

allows me to. Pushing him, he lounges on the bed and I climb up and over him. He's still nude and I have too many clothes on. Standing back up, I pull my dress down my arms and grab my thong as it grazes over my hips. They both land in a heap on the floor. I'm left in my black lace bra and black knee boots. Reaching behind me, with Cruz's eyes following every move, I unhook the bra and let it slither down my arms, before tossing it onto the pile of clothes on the floor. Leaving the boots on, I climb back over him and straddle him. His massive erection is pressed against the wetness at my thighs. Leaning over, I kiss him and he strains up to kiss me back. My hands are braced near his head as I slowly grind against him and feast on his mouth. His hands leave the bed and run up and down my sides… from my hips to the sides of my breasts. My aching breasts. His hands engulf them and he rolls the nipples. I continue to moan into his mouth as we kiss and I create glorious friction down below with my movements.

Breaking the kiss, I trail my lips over his chest, stopping

at his nipples to pay them some attention. They are pebbled, and when my breath grazes them, I feel his cock jerk against me. Reaching down, I grasp him firmly in my hand and use the wetness from myself to stroke him. It's like liquid satin and he's so hard, I can feel the veins pulse in my palm. I have to taste.

My mouth and hair create a devilish trail down his stomach and stop at his hip bones. His "V" is amazing. My tongue licks from one side to the other and with every pass, I get closer and closer to the satiny length in my warm hand. I finally center my mouth over the tip and lick the bead off the tip. I watch his face as I do it. His eyes fly open and he stares at me with hollowed cheeks and gritted teeth. Staring into his eyes, I take his considerable length into my mouth. He's salty and his smell is intoxicating. My hands circle the base as I work the tip and most of the shaft in and out of my warm, wet mouth. His eyes close and his head falls back. I'm getting so turned on with the sounds he's making, moisture is running freely down my thighs.

His moans increase as he pumps his hips in time with my lips. Grabbing my hair, he pulls my mouth off him and pulls me up his body. He flips us and mutters, "I have to be inside you, Tifanie."

His weight is supported by his arms and his face is tight and beautiful with his restraint. Leaning up, I cup his face. I whisper, "So, what are you waiting for?"

His eyes close and he leans into my hand for a brief minute. He takes a deep breath. Opening his eyes, he stares at me. The look in them takes my breath away. He glances at his bedside table as I rub intimately against him.

I make a split second decision. I'm always careful. I'm a paramedic for God's sake, but I'm going with my gut. I speak. "Cruz, I'm safe. I'm on the pill and I'm safe. Are you?"

His eyes search my face and he nods. "I am. I'm tested regularly."

My chest swells and I smile at him. "Good." Wrapping my legs around his waist, I use my hand to guide him to my

143

entrance. "So, take me."

His muttered, "You sure?" is all I need to hear. My nod is lost on a throaty moan as I arch up and he glides in.

His guttural groan fuels the fire and as one, we start to move. He bears down and I arch my back to raise up. My hands travel up his arms and across his chest before circling his back. His pace quickens and I can feel the mattress bounce underneath me as the bed moves. It's fucking amazing.

He slows down and I open my eyes. His face looks tense. I ask, "What's wrong?"

He mutters, "I don't want to hurt you."

Smiling, I slam my pelvis into his; his eyes roll back and he throws his head back. "Ahhhhh."

I love the expression on his face. I repeat my movement and as the sound echoes in the room, he looks down at me. I smile. "I'm not a china doll, Cruz. You can't break me. Do with me what you want. I'm not going anywhere!"

His eyes flash triumph and he starts furiously slamming into me as I match him thrust for thrust. The slapping of flesh and our breathy moans are the only sounds in the room. My nails are raking his back and I'm probably tearing his skin. I've never been fucked like this before. It's hard, rough, and animalistic while still being romantic. It's amazing.

My legs are over his shoulders and he's using them to help propel himself deeper in and out of me. Every glide of his cock is hitting my g-spot from this angle and I'm about to fucking lose my mind. The room starts to spin and my body starts to shake. "Oh Cruz, I need to cum. I'm about to cum. Yes, baby. Give it to me. I want you to give it to me... *YES!!!*"

My head is thrown back against the bed and my nails dig into his back as my thighs clench around his head and I scream out with my release. My release must trigger something in him, because he grabs my hips and anchors me in place as he furiously slams into me. "Tifanie. You feel amazing. You're amazing. Mmmmmmmmm. Ahhhhhhh. *Oh, sh———-hit!*" As he cums, his fingers dig into my hips.

He thrusts a few times and then his body stills as his back

shudders. Slumping over, he rolls so he pulls out of me and falls facedown into the pillow next to me. My pulse is racing and I'm covered in sweat. His. Mine. I don't even know… or care.

Please don't let me wake up. That was insane. My life is forever changed. I knew it would be amazing, but that… that far surpassed all of my many fantasies over the past few months. I want to do it again.

Geez, Tifanie. He just unloaded inside of you. You can barely breathe from the sex and the orgasm. I doubt you'll be able to walk normally tomorrow and you're thinking about doing it again?!

Oh yes, yes I am. I want more…

Turning my head, I look at the gorgeous man next to me and lightly touch the muscles in his back. He jumps and his head turns so he can look at me. I smile softly and he just stares.

My heart drops. He's not regretting what just happened, is he?! He can't!

If he says that he regrets it, I'm going to be crushed.

Don't you dare choose now to wig out, Cruz Edwards!

Chapter Thirteen

Cruz

---

*D*id that just happen? I'm pretty sure I'm having a dream or a fantasy... there is no way that just happened with Tifanie. And if it did, oh my God, I was a crazy person. I was aggressive and rough. I didn't just do that. We didn't just do that. She's going to hate me. I'm just going to lie here.

Her hand on my back has me turning my head. I stare at her. She has a nervous look on her face. *Did I do that? Is she scared of me?!*

I can't look away. She pulls her hand back and sits up as she grabs the sheet and covers her curves with it. I notice the tangled sheets and general mess. We tore this bed up.

Shit!

She picks at the sheet for a minute and then she looks right at me with a challenge in her eyes. "Do you regret what just happened?"

Do I regret what just happened? No. Does she?

I shake my head and sit up with her. I feel uncomfortable with my nakedness and I'm not certain how this conversation is going to go. "No. Do you?"

Her head tilts and her messy hair fans over her shoulders as she scrutinizes me. "No, I don't. Are you sure you're ok with it?"

This feels like a trick question. I don't regret it at all. Not what we did. The sex was phenomenal. I'm just worried I was too much. Too harsh.

"I'm good, Tifanie. Are—are you ok?"

She looks confused. "Am I ok?! Why wouldn't I be ok?"

I shrug and look away from her at the wall where a photo of the bayou is displayed. "I was a little rough. And domineering, Tifanie. I'm sorry."

Her mouth drops open and her expressive hazel eyes

widen. "You're sorry?"

She's just repeating everything I say. What the hell?! She's not ok. Son of a bitch. I knew this wasn't a good idea. That's why I pushed her away...

She grabs my arm and it takes me out of the chaos in my head. Her hand is rubbing my arm. It's soothing. "Cruz, I'm confused. Why are you sorry if you don't regret," she gestures to my destroyed bed, "what just happened with us?"

My head starts pounding. "I don't regret that we slept together, Tifanie. I'm kind of surprised at it to be honest, but I don't regret it. I'm sorry for being rough."

She smiles. "You're sorry for being rough?" I nod. She smirks. "Um, did you miss the moaning and screaming and orgasms you caused?!"

I nervously chuckle. "No, I didn't miss them."

The sheet drops to her waist as she leans over. Her hair tickles my face. She leans down and brushes her mouth across mine. "Well, good. I loved every minute."

Pulling back, I look at her. She seems to be serious. Ok...

"I wasn't too domineering?"

She laughs. "No, you weren't. I'm not really into boring sex." Scooting down, she lies next to me and pats the pillow. I lie down next to her and face her. She scoots over and pushes me so she can lay her chin on my chest as she looks at me. "Cruz, you were assertive. I like it. You're not a Dom by any means. And I'm damn sure not a submissive."

I'm not a what?! "What?"

She giggles. "A Dom. A Dominant."

My brow furrows as I try to process that. "Like whips and chains shit?"

She nods. "Yes, sometimes like that. You aren't that."

How does she know about that? Is that stuff she's into? I'm not... I can't... That's not my thing.

I ask before I can stop myself. "Are you into that?"

She brings her hands to my chest and rests her chin on them as she looks at me. Eventually, after what feels like an hour, she smiles at me. "No. I'm not. I'm not really into being bossed around, in case you hadn't noticed. You are assertive, Cruz, but it's more alpha than dominant and well…" She leans up and bites my chin. "You can be an alpha with me anytime. I find it, and you, extremely sexy."

I feel lighter and she just called me sexy. "I've noticed that about you. And what's the difference between a Dom and an Alpha? Seem the same to me."

She laughs and leans over me, straddling me. "No, not at all. Doms are usually dicks. At least in books. And have Mommy issues. Alphas are just assertive and well… mouth-watering." As she says it, she's running her nails over my chest. She licks her lips as a shudder runs through me, and insanely enough, my dick starts to stir against her. *Already?!*

Putting my hands behind my head, I just look at her. She looks back and then we both smile as she slowly starts to grind against me. I feel coolness against my thighs and realize she still has those knee high boots on. "Your boots are still on."

She laughs musically. "Are they?!" Her eyes are twinkling. "Hmm, I guess I *forgot* to take them off."

My breathing hitches as I feel her moisture against my groin. I mutter, "Forget again."

She grins and reaches between us to once again guide me inside of her. A sigh rolls out of me followed by a groan as she takes control and I let her.

A few hours later, we're lying in a tangle of sheets and legs in my completely messed up bed. I realize it's much later than I thought as the full moon's glow comes through the shades in my bedroom window. I remember she said she had something for me when she texted. The reason for her visit completely slipped my mind in the past few hours' exercise.

Her contented sigh warms my heart and I turn again to glance at her outline in my bed.

She trails her hands over my chest and abs slowly, as if she's memorizing my body. I'm surprisingly comfortable here with her... like this.

Her voice distracts my quaint thoughts. "What are you

thinking?"

What am I thinking? I don't rightly know. I'm thinking I have no idea where to go from here. We just crossed a line with our relationship. I'm thinking I want more of her. But, I'm also thinking I'm not right for her. I can't just change my mindset in a few hours after mind-blowing sex...

I can't tell her any of that though. So instead, I say, "What did you have for me?"

She laughs and leans over me, placing a soft kiss to the underside of my jaw. She murmurs, "Well, um, you got it."

I got it?! What did I get?

Her tongue is running over my jawline and her hands are still on my stomach, inadvertently tracing my washboard abs. Snapping out of the direction of my wayward thoughts, I ask her, "What did I get?"

She nips my chin again and I can see her dark eyes watching my face in the illumination from the moon. "It wasn't exactly as anticipated, but the desired effect was achieved."

My brows furrow in the dark and, as if she knows, her

fingers trace my face. Taking their sweet time, tracing the lines in my forehead. "Me, Cruz. I was going to give you me."

My stomach drops. What does she mean? What is she saying? I know she likes me, but what does she mean? Am I ready for this?! Am I willing, or better yet, am I able to be the man she deserves? The scary fact is that I really don't know...

Chapter Fourteen

Tifanie

Cruz is awfully quiet after my confession. I'm not sure what to think about that. I'm scared to delve in too deeply and spook him, but I don't want any confusion. I know I told him what I want, but he's so new at this. I'm not even certain he wants the same things as me.

I know he wants me. The past few hours have thoroughly demonstrated that, yet, I have no earthly idea if we are wanting the same things.

I can wait. I'm patient. Ok, well I'm really not, but I will be for him. He's worth it to me. I'll do whatever it takes to make him understand that I think he's worth anything. The crazy thing is that if he could even see a fraction of what I see, he'd be completely in love with himself, too.

WAIT! What?! In love!? I'm in love with him?! No, I can't be. We had sex; sex doesn't mean love. I know that. I've had lots of sex with several people, but I never loved any of them…

Shut up, Tifanie. You were in love with Cruz BEFORE you had sex. Now you're just in love with his lovemaking too!

Shit. Shit. Shit.

I sure as hell can't tell him I love him. He'd bolt for sure.

Yes, I'm going to keep on keeping on. I'll be here and be patient, because I DO love him. I love him and he's going to understand he's worthy of that love. To accept my love though, he has to first love himself. So, how exactly do I get him to do that?!

The quiet is making me insane. I decide to be my light, flirtatious self and hopefully calm him down some. His body is so tense I'm scared he's going to jump up and run out of the room.

Leaning over, I lightly kiss his chin. "I like the scruff, Cruz. It's sexy. And you've already had me. Several times." I try to laugh. "No pressure, ok?"

His head turns and though I can't see his eyes, I can feel them on me. "No pressure?" His voice sounds surprised.

I nod though I'm not certain he can see that either. "Yes, no pressure. Ok, so we slept together. But no pressure. I'm not going to chain you down and call you my boyfriend."

He mutters, "I thought you wanted me to be your boy-friend?!" He sounds hurt.

I'm so confused and scared of saying the wrong thing. But I can't really do this. I'm always straightforward. He knows this. I don't want to start sending mixed signals now. Not when we're finally making headway. I decide on total honesty again.

Sitting up, I lean over and turn on his bedside lamp. He blinks in the sudden light. I blink too, but if we're going to talk, like really talk, I'm damn sure not doing it in the freaking dark. I'm not doing it naked either. Looking over, I spot a shirt on a chair. Getting up, I grab it and slip it over my head. It reaches the tops of my thighs. I'm not quite covered, but not naked anymore either.

Sitting back on the bed, I turn and smile at him, hoping to ease his pursed lips and tight expression. He doesn't move, just watches me.

Leaning over, I take his hands in mine and trace the backs with my fingers. "Cruz, I told you what I want. That hasn't changed. If anything, after tonight's events, I want you even more than I did before."

He says flatly, "You just said 'no pressure.' Like you didn't want it anymore."

Cupping his cheek, I lean in and kiss him. His lips are firm and unyielding, but I leave mine on his and brush them back and forth. His lips soften and he kisses me back gently. Smiling against his mouth, I lean back. "Oh, I want it. I want you." His light eyes search my dark ones. "But, I don't want to spook you." His brows furrow again. "Cruz, you are not used to this. Until a few days ago… I'm not certain you ever would have made a move on me. I made the move. I *want* you. I care about you. So much. I don't want to freak you out with my feelings, but I also want you to understand I am not going away. You can push me away. You do push me away. Frequently. You are so damn confusing and frustrating."

He frowns and says, "Hey…"

I put my finger on his lips to silence him. "You are, because for whatever reason, you don't let people in. I know that your mother and what happened to her have something to do with that. I can't imagine what you've had to deal with from people your entire life. People can suck. They can truly suck and can be mean and hateful.

"I know this. I see some of the darkest things imaginable in my line of work, but I also see some of the most beautiful and amazing.

"I know that you know I have money. I come from money. BUT… you know me. I'm not the name. I'm not the person who will ever judge you. Judge anyone. I don't do that. And I care about you.

"You… you're special, Cruz Edwards. You mean something… to me. And you can push… you can try to run…

but I'm not letting you." I smirk at the complexity of the emotions in his beautiful eyes. "You messed up."

He exclaims, "I messed up?"

I nod. "Yup. You did. You told me you wanted me. You just showed me you want me. You tried to push me away because you were worried you weren't good enough." Leaning my forehead against his, I mutter as I look into his eyes, "That shows me you're good enough. You've always been good enough. You messed up. You told me you cared. And I care too, so that means... you're stuck with me."

He stares at me and I hold my breath. Groaning, he grabs the back of my head and pulls me the rest of the way into him. He kisses me until my toes curl.

When we stop and come up for air, I take a long deep breath. He's quiet again.

"You ok?"

He props a pillow behind his back and sits against the headboard. He pulls me against him and I rest my head against his hard chest, listening to the rapid beats of his heart.

His voice rumbles in his chest as he says, "There's more. To the story."

Turning my head, I look up at him. "Ok, so tell me. If you want to. I'm here."

He nods and looks down at me. "Ok." Taking a tortured breath, he starts, "The man who fathered me is a rapist. I told you that."

I nod but stay silent.

"He's been in jail since he was convicted. I'm twenty-five years old. He's been in jail for that long. He beat and raped my momma and staged it to look like a robbery. She got pregnant and kept me. She raised me all by herself. She doted on me. The baby from a man who assaulted her. It's always just been the two of us. It wasn't easy. She was a young black woman and I'm a mixed child who came from a rape, but she's never held that against me. Even when people were horrible to her, she tried to protect me.

"About a year ago, I got a call from the prison. *He* was

coming up for parole. I was told that *he* had been a model prisoner for years and had found Jesus and was remorseful for his crimes. They said he'd served his time.

"I didn't care. I don't care. I don't buy it. I'm sorry, but I don't.

"A little after that, *he* started contacting me. He'd send letters and every few weeks, he'd call. Now, he'd never, not once, contacted me before. I answered the call the first time. I don't even know how he got my number. It's private and unlisted. I hung up when he said who he was and that he wanted to meet me.

"He kept calling. He'd leave messages on my machine and he kept sending the letters asking for me to please meet with him. He claims he wants to meet his *son*. Only, I'm *not* his son. He's not my father. I don't have a father and I have no desire or intention of meeting him. As far as I care, he's dead.

"So, he contacted my momma."

I gasp. He contacted Cruz's mother?! How is that even possible? Why is that allowed?!

He laughs. It's harsh. "Yeah, can you believe that!? He called my momma and asked her to please talk to me and get me to meet with him. He called the woman he *RAPED* because I don't want to have anything to do with him.

"I told her no. I'm not doing that. I don't want to and I'm scared that if I do, I'll fly into a rage."

I take his hand and hold it tightly. He looks at me and his eyes are full of pain.

"He hurt my momma, Tif. She endured so much shit because of what he did and then because of me. It's his fault. I don't want to meet him. I don't want to know him. I don't get why he wants to know me. I don't buy it."

I can completely understand why Cruz doesn't want to meet the man who fathered him. My heart is aching for him and his mother. I wish I knew what to say or what to do. Is there anything I can do?!

But the thing I'm really not understanding is if he thinks this new information is supposed to change anything. I love him. He doesn't know that, but I love him.

I'm going to be here. I love him and I'm not going anywhere. I'm here for him and all of his demons. They don't matter to me…

Chapter Fifteen

Cruz

I've just spilled everything. I told Tifanie everything. She's so quiet. Is she going to walk out? Is she going to say anything?

I've never told anyone about that stuff. Just Dade. The guys know about what happened to my momma and Clove knows because we grew up together and she was always a friend, but I've never shared that information with anyone other than them.

This is a first… I wish she'd say something.

Eventually, she lifts her head and stares at me. She smiles. "Thank you for sharing that with me. I am so glad that you did."

Is that it?

She presses a soft kiss against the cross tattoo on my bicep. That tattoo is for my momma for everything she's done for me, for her unwavering faith in both me and the higher power she's taught me about my entire life. My heart swells as I feel the light pressure from Tifanie's lips against the one thing that reminds me every single day of the sacrifices my amazing momma made for me.

Laying her head back against my chest, she murmurs quietly, "I can understand your hesitation about his intentions. I happen to agree with you. If what you say is true, then he seems to be pushing. If he genuinely wanted to get to know you, then I would think he would respect your boundaries and the fact that you are not reciprocating. I agree that it seems as if he has ulterior motives."

That is such a relief to hear someone else agree with me. My arm snakes around Tif and I flip her onto her back. She looks up at me with surprise. Leaning down, I kiss her as my hands trail over her thighs and start to push up my shirt.

She grins. "Again, Superman?"

I can't help it. I grin back. I feel suddenly lighter. "I do have something that feels like steel right now."

She laughs and her legs wraps around my waist.

For the next hour, we lose the ability to speak and the only sounds in the room are breathy moans and uttered shouts before we eventually fall asleep entwined in each other's arms.

An annoying sound wakes me from my relaxed slumber. What is that weight on my legs?

Opening my eyes, I see the wavy brown hair on the pillow next to me. Sleepy hazel eyes are watching me and the weight on my legs is removed. The sound comes again. Tifanie groans and stretches. "Ugh, I think that's my phone. What time is it?"

Rolling, I glance at the clock on the nightstand. Is that the time?! "Is it really 10AM?"

She mutters, "Shit!" and hops out of bed to search

through the clothes on the floor. She comes up with her phone and grimaces as she checks the caller ID. "Hey. Sorry, I'm running late... Yes, I'll come grab you... No, I'm not at home... Yes, I'm at Cruz's... Shut the hell up. Don't be an ass... Yeah, I'll call you when I'm on my way... Shut up!"

Her cheeks are pink as she hangs up. Who the hell was on the phone?!

Looking at me over her shoulder, she says sheepishly, "Ty." My brow arches. Why is she going to go get Ty on her day off? What the hell?

She looks at me for a minute and then slyly says, "What are you doing today?"

What am I doing today? What the hell? "Nothing. No plans. Why?"

She purses her lips and stares at me. She looks nervous. She walks across the bedroom and plops onto the bed. "Well... Ty and I are heading to Chateau du Bellaforte."

My eyes widen and my mouth drops open. "Ok..."

She clutches her chest and says really fast, "So, do you

want to come with me? I know it's crazy and we aren't like together or anything, but Ty is coming too, as a buffer because my family sucks for the most part. They throw rich men that my father thinks are suitable husbands at me left and right. No matter how many I blow off, there are always more. But, it's my grandma's birthday and I do love my grandma. She's the best. So, do you want to come?"

What did she say? She wants me to go with her to a family event? At her family's mansion?! *With her family?* That girl from the elevator? As what? She just said we're not together, so what the hell?

I mutter, "What? Why do you want me to come?"

She looks at me through her lashes and bites her lip. I've never seen her nervous before. "Well, because I care about you. You don't have to. I know you're not like my... beau, but well, if you don't have plans... You could come."

"Sometimes, you speak very... rich. Did you know that? Do you want me to come?"

She frowns and nods as she chews on her lip. "Ugh and I

do. I would love it if you'd come."

This is it. The moment of truth. What am I going to do? Am I going to take a chance with her or am I going to do what I always do and push people away?!

The truth is, I'm scared to death. Tifanie and her family are rich and powerful. I'm rich too, but it's not the same thing. I took a chance last night and she and I *ARE* in a relationship. We've been in a relationship. Yet, now I'm wanting to take the chance. I want to *be* in a relationship… with her. She fights for me… She pushes me… She makes me better. I want to take a chance for her, but more importantly, I think it's time I take a chance *for me.*

I make the choice. This is the start of a whole new chapter. Rubbing my jaw, I watch her watch me. Finally, I nod. "Ok, then I'll go."

Her shock is palpable. "You will?"

Chuckling, I pull her to me. She falls across the bed. "I will." Kissing her softly, I pull back and look at her. "Oh, and Tifanie?"

She squints at me and asks quietly, "Yeah?"

I mutter against her mouth, "I am your beau."

She jerks back and almost tumbles to the floor. I grab her arm at the last second and laugh at the look of complete and utter shock on her face.

"Careful, there. You almost fell off the bed."

Nodding, a smile lights up her face. "You're my boy-friend?"

Standing up, I pull her with me and set her on her feet. "I guess so. Since I can't get rid of you and all… So, what am I wearing to this party?"

Her smile warms the whole room and my chest feels full.

She helps me find clothes and we shower together before we head to her house so she can get ready and change her clothes.

About an hour later, we're heading down Highway 1 in West Baton Rouge, on the other side of the river, where Chateau du Bellaforte is located and has been for the past two hundred years.

We stopped by Ty's on the way out and picked him up. To say he was surprised to see me in the car is a bit of an understatement. His mouth hit the ground before he slapped me on the back and chuckled as he climbed into the back seat.

Tifanie and Ty are giving me a lesson on her family on the drive. We're driving down the road and I'm looking at all of the sugar cane fields. I'm not used to seeing so much cane. I didn't think there were still fields this large anymore. We pass an old sugar mill and the smoke-stack looks to be freshly painted. Cinclaire is in bold black letters against the pristine white. It's so pretty out here.

Eventually, we turn off the highway and cross the train tracks; we're on a private road that is made of dirt and limestone. I'm just starting to wonder where exactly we're going and if this road actually leads anywhere when tall, majestic gates come into view.

My head is spinning with all of the information I've been given on the drive over. I'll never in a million years remember this shit.

Ty sees me messing with the collar of my button up shirt and laughs. He mutters, "Just remember, they're all snobs and won't like you anyway, no matter what you do, so as snobby as they are, act twice as indifferent."

My eyes fly to him and Tif softly smiles. "He's right." She reaches for my hand across the console and squeezes. "Seriously, don't even worry about them. They won't like you. They don't like me. They like puppets with money. If you're not like them, they don't like you. It's really that simple and ridiculous. I don't care. So, you don't care either. Screw them." Bringing my hand to her mouth, she kisses my fingers and laughs. "Seriously, fuck them. They're all snobby idiots."

Ty claps my shoulder. "Honestly, man. Unless you are exactly like them, they'll look down at you. Just don't let them get to you. Or be like me and do everything you can to piss them off. I love that shit. They hate me anyway, so why not?!"

I look at him as Tif drives down a road between trees through ornate gardens that seem to stretch a mile in either direction. "You've been to a lot of these with her?"

He grins. "Quite a few. I never send her to these by herself. They throw rich tools at her left and right. I've always been the buffer. Well, for the past few years anyway." He laughs. "Now that's your job. I'm just going to hang out with Ms. Clarabelle and soak it in as she pisses people off." My look of surprise makes him laugh even more. "Seriously, she's awesome. Tif takes after her, which is awesome! She doesn't filter at all and she's old and rich so no one dares say anything to her. It's greatness. You never know what's going to come out of her mouth."

He whistles and I turn. He mutters, "Check that shit out."

My mouth hangs open. I blink, but nope it's still there. Holy shit. That's a house?!

I've never seen a house like that in my life. I've been to plantations before, but holy shit. Tifanie *lived* here?! Her family lives here? The grounds are insane, but the house takes the cake. It's huge and breathtaking. It screams money. I'm immediately ready to tell her to turn the car around.

The house is a crisp white with lots of white columns set under towering oak trees. I don't even know how many sets of French doors and balconies I'm looking at. The porch area in front of the house is the size of my entire house and my house is not small.

Jeez…

Tifanie stops to the side of the driveway and pulls under some trees. She grimaces as she turns the car off and says, "Ok, y'all ready?" She squeezes my hand one more time. I turn away from the house and look at her with apprehension. She can read the distress in my face. "It's just a house, Cruz. It's gorgeous though, huh?!"

She thinks this is "just a house?!"

I nod. What else can I do?! I'm here now, too late to leave. The porch is packed with people standing around drinking out of what looks like crystal glasses and flutes. The front door opens and even more people come out of the house. Everyone appears to be staring at the car. The men are all in dress coats and slacks and the ladies are in dresses. Are they wearing hats?!

What the hell did I get myself into?

Tifanie smiles reassuringly at me and opens the door. As she stands up, she leans back in and says, "Welcome to hell. Otherwise known as a Saturday with the Bellafortes."

Ty laughs heartily and calls out, "Where's the alcohol?"

Taking a deep breath and wondering what in the ever loving hell I'm even doing here, I get out. Under the un-blinking stares of everyone on the porch, the three of us head to the house.

Tifanie stops. I stop with her and she places her hand on my face. She leans up and brushes her mouth against my lips gently. Then, linking her fingers with mine, she pulls my reluctant body toward the house and says with a forced smile, "Ready to be judged?"

Chapter Sixteen

Tifanie

As we get out of the car, the family and guests pile onto the porch and I can clearly see them staring, gesturing, and whispering. I can't imagine what they're saying about Cruz. It automatically pisses me off and I kick myself for subjecting him to the hell he's about to encounter.

What was I thinking asking him to accompany me here? These people are hateful and shallow and stuck up.

Ugh, I can't believe I'm doing this to him. This is my family. I HAVE to be around them occasionally, but he doesn't, and I brought him straight into the lion's den... like fresh meat on a platter... Son of a bitch.

Ty just strolls up the steps and heads straight to Grandma Clarabelle in her chair. He kisses her cheek and she reaches up to hug him as he says something that makes heads turn sharply toward them. Then, they both laugh and glance at Cruz and me. Ty winks and snags a glass of what looks like bourbon from a passing tray. He downs the entire thing and signals for the waiter to hand him another one.

Good thinking, Ty. I want one, too. Or ten.

Cruz mutters under his breath, "Everyone is staring at me. And your sister is glaring."

I look to the right of the porch. Yup, AnnaBeth is indeed glaring and the scowl on her face is almost comical. The perfectly pressed idiot next to her is glaring too and I don't miss the clenching of his hands at his sides.

Fucking seriously.

Scouring the porch, I see my parents encircled by their friends and they are all staring with looks of blatant disapproval at my hand grasped in Cruz's.

Get over it!

Gently pulling Cruz along with me, we make our way to

the porch. Grandma Clarabelle calls out to us, "My favorite grand-daughter is here." Everyone gasps. She continues as if she didn't hear them. "Come here, Tifanie. Ty tells me this is your gentleman. Let me have a look at him. He looks mighty nice from this distance."

I chuckle. Cruz pulls back against my hand... And the whispering escalates.

Winking at him, I say out of the corner of my mouth, "Grandma Clarabelle is a mess."

He nods but looks completely uncomfortable.

We head across the painted wooden beams and people purposely step out of the way to make certain they don't touch us. The whispering follows closely behind. My back is ramrod straight and I can feel the unmistakable burn of rage pulsing down my spine. I try to ignore it and push it down. I don't want Cruz to see my fury unleashed.

Grandma Clarabelle focuses her dark brown gaze on us as we approach. Her face gives nothing away.

Leaning down, I kiss her leathery cheek. Her hand reaches out and traces my cheekbone. "Bonjour, ma belle-fille." As she smiles at me, her face is instantly transformed and you can clearly see what a beauty she once was.

Leaning back, I smile back. "Bonjour, grand-mere. C'est Cruz… Mon petit ami." I glance at him and see him staring at me. I smile.

He looks at Grandma. Holding out his hand, he takes Grandma Clarabelle's in his. "Hello, Ma'am. Thank you for having me today. Happy birthday."

She yanks on his hand. He looks at me sharply. I smile and nod. Grandma Clarabelle says, "Come on down here. I can't see as well as I once could. I want to get a good look at you. Tifanie doesn't bring gentlemen around these snobs very often." She inclines her head around her and everyone sputters. She cackles. I can see Cruz hiding a smirk. "Not that I blame her. Ty here doesn't count. He's not romantically interested in her.

"My grand-daughter is very special. *Ma belle fleur forte.* My beautiful strong flower. She's a feisty one. Like me. But these sticks-in-the-mud want to try to tame her. I can't tell them enough you can't tame a wild stallion and why would you want to?!

"There are enough stuffed shirts around this *maison*. And these women like to walk around like they're wearing corsets and sipping tea. It bores me to tears."

I am grinning like a fool at her words. I love that she doesn't mince them. I get my bluntness from her. I love that quality.

My father steps up and coughs to get our attention. He stiffly kisses the air at my cheek while my mother trails behind him, clutching her pearls and looking at Cruz like she thinks he's going to rape and pillage the women at the party.

I roll my eyes.

Father flatly says, "Hello, Tifanie. We weren't certain you would make it today. I've called several times but haven't received a return call. Are you going to introduce us to your... *friend*?"

Taking a step back toward Cruz and wrapping my arm

around his waist, I look at both of my parents and the crowd watching us with rapt fascination. With just as much formality, I answer him, "Hello, Father. This is my boyfriend, Cruz Edwards. Cruz, my father, Senator Richmond Bellaforte. That's my mother, Rosalind Bellaforte, next to him."

Father stiffly holds his hand out to shake Cruz's and my mother's lips are white they're pursed so tightly.

Ty calls out, "Y'all know me. No introductions needed."

A few people chuckle, but most are just staring and not so silently judging.

Cruz firmly shakes my father's hand and nods at my mother. "It's nice to meet you both. You have a beautiful home."

A rude curse and a mocking chuckle interrupt the tenseness on the porch. The idiot next to my sister speaks, "Yes, it is a gallant home. I'm certain it's overwhelming for you. I doubt you're used to this level of class. People unlike us are usually in awe."

My gaze snaps to him and I mutter a curse of my own as

I glare at him and my sister. Before I can unleash my wrath on them both, Ty speaks up dryly. "Stanton, I'd say I'm surprised at your audacity, but shit, let's face it... I'm not. You're a pompous ass. I mean what kind of man proposes to one sister and when she flatly refuses, immediately starts courting the *other* sister?! Yet, you speak of class?!" He insultingly tips his glass at Stanton and AnnaBeth. "By the way, that man you're trying to insult is not an idiot and is, believe it or not, a celebrity. In fact... I bet if you combined all of you stuffed shirts and your supporters from this magnificent gala, more people would know who *he* is over all of you."

Cruz quickly looks at me with a question before looking at Ty in appreciation while I also smile at him with unsurpassed glee. He pops a cherry into his mouth as he says, "Oh, was that rude?! Oops, my bad. I think I need another drink." He winks at AnnaBeth and Stanton who are both standing there with rage on their faces. "How about I grab you one, AnnaBeth? You're looking a little peaked. Might take the edge off and remove that stick from your ass."

Grandma Clarabelle guffaws with laughter and calls out to Ty to grab her a glass of champagne. She looks at Anna-Beth and says, "That man is what you need, child... not that weasel beside you."

AnnaBeth glares at me and stomps into the house muttering about the classlessness of some people with Stanton shooting daggers in our direction as he trails behind her. I roll my eyes as everyone glares at me and Cruz.

My parents turn swiftly on their heels and silently follow my sister and her fiancé into the house.

Turning to Cruz, I ask with false cheerfulness, "Having fun yet?"

He looks like he's having a hard time with it all, so I take his hand and pull. Grandma Clarabelle says, "Take him into the maze. Get some air and get away from all this ridiculousness, ma belle. I may have Ty escort me to meet up with you in a bit if I feel up to the walk."

Smiling and nodding, I pull a silent Cruz with me and

head in the direction of the maze. A waiter passes us on the steps and I snag a drink and tell Cruz to grab one too. He does.

We leave the crowd behind and stroll through the meticulous rose gardens as I head in the direction of the maze and sip my drink. The entrance to the maze is a jasmine-covered pergola with benches underneath it. I stop and sit down. Cruz doesn't sit, he just stares off into the distance. The property is over five hundred acres and stretches as far as the eye can see and well beyond.

I feel awful. I would like to say I'm surprised that Cruz was treated like that by the people attending this soiree, but I would be lying. I don't know what to say though. For the first time in my life I can remember, I'm speechless. I do need to explain about Stanton though.

He doesn't speak, but I see him take deep breaths. Standing, I walk behind him and place my hand on his back. He freezes at the contact. Leaning my front against his back, I whisper, "I'm sorry. I need to explain about the Stanton thing."

Turning his head, he looks down at me. "He proposed to you?"

I laugh harshly. "He did. But we *never* dated. Like ever." Cruz looks at me like he's not certain he believes me. "No, I swear. We never did anything. We grew up together. His father is in politics as well. We were thrown together our whole lives, yet I was never interested in him. Last Christmas, at the holiday party, he proposed. Out of the blue. I was shocked. I said no. Why would I marry him? I can't even stand him. He was pissed and tried a couple of more times. I refused and the next thing I know, he's dating AnnaBeth. Now they're engaged. Neither is even interested in the other, yet they're going to get married... Yeah, that's going to work out brilliantly.

"Yet, it's what my father wanted... a union between our families, so of course AnnaBeth will do it. She's the perfect daughter. Always doing whatever is needed. Whatever she's told."

He's staring at me. "Wow. I didn't realize that shit still happened. Is it always like that? Are they always like that?"

I laugh and nod. "Yup. It does. Old South… And yeah, they are."

He shudders. "That's terrible. I can't believe they treat you like that." His hands clench and unclench. "No one should be treated like that. Especially not you."

Does he hear what he's saying? No one *should* be treated like that. He's right. But that includes himself. Does he even know what he's saying?

Leaning up, I kiss his back through his shirt and wrap my arms around his stomach. "I don't care about the way they treat me. They've done that my whole life. I'm not like them and they hate it. But I don't care. I'm me. I live my life the way I want. I do what makes me happy. My grandma has always been in my corner. I'm so like her. I think that's another reason they dislike me so intensely. I don't follow their rules. I don't find the stupid things important that they do." He rests his hand over the top of mine. "Honestly, I don't care about what they think about me. I'm used to it and I swear to you I don't care. None of that fazes me. But I'm so angry at the way they treated you."

He turns away and looks out at the property. Staring at the trees in the distance, he swallows. "Tifanie, I've been treated like I was worthless, like I don't fit in anywhere, my whole life. It's nothing new to me. But unlike you, it does bother me. I don't want you to have to deal with the shit that just happened because of me. That's the last thing I want."

Grabbing his face, I pull it down to mine. "Cruz, the fact that you're here with me right now… that you just went through that bullshit with my family, that you're here with me right this second… I would deal with any of those idiots one hundred times if I could have this."

He groans and grabs my hips, pulling me into his body. He backs me into the side of the pergola and the jasmine surrounds us as he captures my mouth. His tongue sweeps past my lips and tangles with mine as my hands grasp at his back and neck, holding on for dear life.

I'm pressed against the jasmine, crushing it. The smell weaves around us, as we forget the rest of the world. The only thing that exists is he and I, right here, right now, in the sunlight and jasmine.

Chapter Seventeen

Cruz

I'm pressing Tifanie into the jasmine, kissing her in a way I've never kissed a woman before. Every time we move, the jasmine releases its heady fragrance. It's like heady incense and it's completely intoxicating. The smells combined with the taste of her mouth and the softness of her lips and tongue as she moves sensuously against me and lets out delicious moans, transports me to another place.

It's like we're in our own world out here, away from everyone. No judgments, no rules, just the wondrous feelings associated with the woman in my arms.

Her breathy moans have me rock hard and her gentle swaying presses her perfect curves against me in all the right places.

Remembering where we are, and who's at this party, has me reluctantly pulling back from her. She doesn't let me get far. Her arms weave around me and hold me close as my hands almost claw her hips with the urgency of my restraint. All I want to do is raise her skirt and bury myself inside her warm, willing softness, yet I know I can't do it. Not here. Not with these people around.

I've never had a woman stir my senses the way Tifanie does. I've never wanted to just let go of everything and just… be. But I do. With Tifanie, I do.

It's damn frightening.

Her mouth is trailing over my jaw and up to my ear as her breath fuels my passion. I'm forcing myself to stop from touching her inappropriately, yet it's the hardest thing I've ever done.

She leans into my ear and sucks my pierced lobe into her mouth. Her tongue is flicking against the diamond stud and her warm, wet breath is torturing me. Her breathy voice is in my ear. "I want you to take me, Cruz."

Leaning back, I look at her. Her lips are swollen and lush and her eyes are dark and glazed. She's gorgeous. She's so passionate and wanton and it's for me… I'm not certain how to handle that. I'm not certain why I deserve her and everything she's offering.

I want to indulge her, but I can't. Not here.

"I can't take you. Not here. Not outside. Not like this. I won't do anything to jeopardize you, Tifanie."

She sighs. "Screw these people." But she leans back. "You're too scrumptious. I want you. I want you to take me. I want to take you. I'm so wet right now."

My eyes widen at her declaration. I smirk. "Yeah? How wet?"

The gleam in her eyes brightens and she grabs my hand and pulls me into the maze. Chuckling, I follow her. She seems to know exactly where she's going, so I just hold on. We turn one more corner and she smirks at me before she ducks through a small, almost invisible gap in the hedges.

She pulls against my hand and says from the other side, "Come on. Hurry."

Why not?!

I push through and look around. We're in a little clearing. There's a small fountain and some wildflowers cover the lush grass. It's beautiful. It's small, only about twelve feet wide and almost a circle.

Turning, I take in the entire secret garden in the maze. As I come full circle, my gaze centers on Tifanie. She's staring at me with a sexy smile as she drops the black dress to the ground. She's in nothing but her light blue panties and bra. She's already kicked off her shoes.

Her finger beckons to me and, as if I'm a puppet on a string, I cross the short distance to her. As I reach her, I huskily whisper, "What are you doing, Tifanie?"

She leans up and wraps her arms around my neck as she stands on her tiptoes to brush her lips against mine softly before whispering, "Exactly what I want to."

Groaning, I grab her and cup her ass through her panties.

She hops up and wraps her legs around my waist. Her mouth is once again on my ear. "Why don't you see just how wet?"

She's crazy. We're in a secret garden in a maze at her family's mansion and there are people who dislike me everywhere, yet, I can't deny her. Setting her on her feet, I kneel and look up at her. The sun is behind her, so she's got almost a halo around her head and her beauty astounds me.

This woman wants me. She's offering herself to me. Her family hates me and she doesn't care.

My hands trail up her thighs and stop at her hips. I take in the darkness of my skin against the olive skin of her hips. She doesn't care. She accepts me for me. She's fought for me. I realize the treasure that she is and it's like a lightbulb goes off. She's mine.

The satin of her panties almost floats down her legs and joins the dress at her feet. She reaches back and unhooks her bra. She's completely nude before me in the glow of the sun. Grabbing her, I lean my head into her stomach and just hug her tightly.

Her hand touches my head and cradles it before turning my face up to look at her. She kneels down before me. Her husky whisper wakes me up. "You have far too many clothes on, Cruz."

I do have too many clothes on. Her smaller hands help my large ones as we unbutton my shirt before slipping it off my shoulders and down my arms. Her mouth follows the trail of the shirt and stops at my waistband. Before I can unbuckle it, her hands have accomplished the task and she's reaching into my slacks and encircling me. My head falls back and I moan.

Her hands are soft and warm against my steely hardness. She gently rubs the tip and my eyes snap open.

The undiluted pleasure on her face just from touching me is my undoing. Pulling back, I quickly remove my slacks. Within seconds, I'm just as naked as she is. Using my shirt as a blanket, I spread it out and lay her back against it. The sun is kissing her skin and it appears to be glowing. I can almost believe she's a mythical creature.

Smiling at me she says, "Are you just going to look at me, Cruz?" Her hands trail over the curves of her body and I can't look away. "I think you're supposed to be checking something." She slowly spreads her legs and I focus on the shimmering pink folds nestled there.

Swallowing, I look away from the slick treasure trove below and focus on her face. Her cheeks are pink and her eyes are dilated with intense passion. Reaching out, my hands trail up her calves and over her thighs before stopping at the juncture there. Watching her face, I slowly run my fingers through the wetness. She moans and her legs fall further apart.

I want to dive in, but I'm still worried about someone seeing us out here. We're in the open.

As if she can read my mind, she closes her legs, trapping my hand. "No one knows this is here. It's my secret place. No one is going to see us." Her come-hither smile is my undoing.

I start to move my fingers and she opens her legs again. I'm fascinated with my dark fingers disappearing into her pink folds. She's gripping me and pulling at me. Her head is thrown back and her neck is arched. She's gorgeous.

Her moans are making me twitch and my cock is jerking in time to them.

She looks at me. "Lie back."

She wants me to lie back? What?

Pulling away from me, she sits up. I feel the loss of her warmth immediately. Pointing to my shirt, she says again, "Lie back."

I don't argue. I lie back and she leans over me and tickles my abdomen with her hair. Her head is millimeters above my skin, so she's not touching me, but her breath is an intimate caress. It's strangely erotic and gives me goose bumps.

My eyes close as her hair whispers against my skin. She stops and my eyes flash open. My cock is jutting out proudly and she's over it, just looking down. Her lips are moist from her tongue but her eyes rise to mine. As they meet, she leans down and takes me into her mouth. Watching myself become engulfed by her lips is quite possibly the single hottest thing I have ever seen. Still watching me, she starts to move. Her mouth is gliding over me and my hips automatically move in time with her suction.

My hands weave through her hair and guide her mouth at the speed I want. It's too much. I'm going to blow.

Releasing her hair, I pull back and the suction makes a popping sound as she releases me from her mouth. She smiles as she straddles me. I'm so hard and she's so wet, no guidance is needed. I slip inside of her with no assistance. We both groan as I settle home.

She starts to move and I help. Within seconds the sound of slapping flesh is echoing throughout the clearing. She's moaning so loudly, I'm certain they can hear it at the house. I sit up and take her mouth to try to quiet her some as she rides me.

Our mouths and tongues are in perfect sync with our

fucking and the combined sensations have both of us on the brink within minutes.

She bites my tongue as she shatters around me and her spasms send me over the edge as well. I roar into her mouth and she swallows it.

My body is jerking and convulsing and I shoot streams of semen into her. I wonder where it's all coming from. Finally, I'm spent. She leans her forehead against mine and I open my eyes.

She stays in my lap while I soften inside of her and she takes my mouth in another sweet and gentle kiss. Her hands cradle my face. Mine mimic her stance and my hands are buried in her hair as we kiss and our heartbeats return to normal. Her breasts are against my chest.

Eventually, she leans back and takes a deep breath. I lean back on my hands and she smiles at me. "Wow, Cruz."

She makes me smile. "Wow, yourself."

She rakes her nails gently down my stomach and the muscles jump. She smirks. "You're so fucking sexy. You make me crazy. You know that?"

I think about it for a second. I like that I make her crazy. The fact that I, Cruz Edwards, make this amazing woman lose her mind... that's kind of a good feeling. It's an unexpected feeling, but a damn good one.

This is too good to be true. Tifanie is too good to be true. Too good for me anyway. Shut up, Cruz. Just enjoy it. She cares about you. Stop looking for reasons to run.

For once, I want to defeat the urge to run... I want to stay. Right here. With Tifanie.

Chapter Eighteen

Tifanie

I'm speechless. Again. I have nothing in my brain, no thought of speech. Dear lord, Cruz is perfection. He's freaking amazing and he deserves the platinum record for lovemaking.

Best. Sex. Ever. In. The. History. Of. The. World!

And mine! Finally, all mine! Hallelujah!

I just seduced Cruz in my secret garden. This was always my place. My special place. When things would get insane and my family would get to be too much... I would come here. No one knows about it. Just me. I found it when I was six. I've never shared it with anyone before. It was always my secret place. My sacred space. Now, I've shared it with Cruz...

We're still naked and I flop down next to him on the crushed flowers. I want to stay here forever… in my secret garden, but alas we can't. There's a party up at the house and my family is also there. Reluctantly, I sit up and search out my clothes. I can feel his gaze on me as I crawl across the crushed wildflowers to grab my undergarments. Standing, I turn and look at him as I slip into my panties. He just watches me with his hand shielding his eyes from the sun.

He looks content. He looks… happy.

"You're too much, Tifanie."

I smile. "No, I'm just enough."

He smiles back as he stands and stretches. His skin is gleaming in the reflection of the sun. He's so defined. His body is perfection, but then you add in that face and those eyes and I have no defense. I'm just a goner. Is there any wonder I'm completely in love with him?!

Stop that right now. If he had any idea on what you're thinking, he'd be out of here faster than Usain Bolt!

Baby steps. All in good time, Tifanie!

He smirks at me as he slips his slacks back on. "What's that look for? What's going through that head of yours?"

Chuckling, I take in the picture of him with his slacks unbuttoned standing in front of me in my favorite place. Holding out my hands like a camera, I wink at him. "More than you want to know."

Smiling, he slips his shirt back on and starts on the buttons. I just watch him, as that body I'm fascinated by, is covered back up. He stops and rolls the sleeves before he tucks the tail back in and buckles his belt. I'm so distracted by him I completely stop getting dressed as I watch him.

A voice suddenly approaches the clearing. Putting my finger over my lips, I stare at him to convey that he should be quiet.

He nods as they get closer. I slip my dress on and listen to see who it is. My sister's voice comes through loud and clear. It sounds as if she's on the phone. I don't hear anyone else. "I don't know what Tifanie was thinking bringing him here. She's always snubbing her nose at us. I'm so embarrassed. Why can't she ever think of anyone but herself?

"That… *man*… He's black! Why would she do that? She can't really be interested in him!"

How dare she?! How dare she say that! Stupid bitch! I'm furious and I want nothing more than to storm out of here and light into her.

Cruz reads my face and shakes his head to stop me. He shrugs and smiles at me. *Wait, is he ok?! He's not pissed that she just said that?!*

I look at him questioningly. He smiles and crosses over to me as AnnaBeth's voice slowly gets farther away. She's still close, but no longer right on top of us. Taking me in his arms, he leans down and kisses me softly. I look at him in wonder. I whisper, "What was that?"

He smiles and brushes his mouth against mine again before whispering back, "Just kissing my amazing girlfriend."

My heart seems to lighten and I'm surprised I don't float off the ground. Wrapping my arms around his neck, I pull his head back down to me and kiss him with all of the pent up emotions I'm feeling. I put all of the love in my heart into my kiss and tell him without words just what he means to me.

We only break apart as we hear more footsteps on the path. Both of us listen. These are fast and seem angry.

A voice cuts off AnnaBeth's conversation. "What the hell are you doing, AnnaBeth?!"

She shrieks and something falls to the path. "Jesus! What the hell? What am I doing?! What the hell are *you* doing? Are you *following* me?!"

Looking at Cruz, my shock must be comical on my face. That's Ty!

We hear a slight struggle and then a curse. "Yes, I am. I cannot believe you just allowed that douche canoe to say those things about Cruz! You're such a piece of work, AnnaBeth Bellaforte!"

Her enraged voice spits out, "I'm a piece of work?! Me?! I'm not the one making a spectacle of myself! I'm not the one parading my lover around father's constituents just to embarrass my family!"

"No, you would never do anything to *embarrass* the family, now would you?! You're so worried about what *daddy* thinks that you don't give a damn about anyone else. The perfect princess!"

Her painful gasp shakes me to my core. What the hell?!

"Go to hell, Ty! You don't know anything! You go to hell!" Her voice cracks before her footsteps recede rapidly.

The hedges rattle as if someone hit them and Ty mutters, "I'm already there, princess! I'm already there." before he stomps farther down the path as well.

My sister and Ty?! What the shit did we just hear?!

My eyes are shocked as I glance at Cruz. I whisper, "That was my sister... and... Ty!"

He looks at me wryly. "Yeah, I gathered that too."

"What the fuck?!"

He grimaces. "I have no idea, Tif. I don't know." Taking my hand, he squeezes my fingers. "We should get back to the party."

I nod. My sister and Ty… The fuck!?

We head to the party and for the next few hours, we mingle and eat and drink. I keep an eye out for AnnaBeth and Ty, but both keep their distance. AnnaBeth stays at Stanton's side and Ty stays near Grandma Clarabelle putting away a good amount of liquor.

We sing Happy Birthday and a giant cake is brought out and consumed. Grandma Clarabelle talks to Cruz and laughs a lot. She seems to like him.

The party wraps up as it starts to get dark and my parents head inside to change clothes for some fundraiser they are attending. AnnaBeth disappears with Stanton and eventually it's just Grandma Clarabelle, myself, and Cruz. Ty is passed out on the sofa in the den. He drank a lot of alcohol.

After checking his phone, Cruz excuses himself to make a phone call and it's just Grandma Clarabelle and me in the parlor. Grandma orders tea and I ask for a coffee and the housekeeper heads off to fix it. We sit in comfortable silence for a bit.

Grandma breaks the silence. "So, dear. You're in love."

My gaze swings to her and I laugh at the expression on her face. I'm not going to lie to her. Glancing at the door to make certain Cruz is not there, I nod. "I am."

She chuckles as she sees my glance. "You don't want him to know. He's got some things with him. Some secrets."

I shrug. "He has some stuff, yes. But, no secrets. I know about everything."

She nods and leans her head back against the velvet chair. "He's a beautiful man with a wonderful demeanor. He's good for you, belle fleur." The housekeeper quietly delivers our tray of refreshments and excuses herself from the room once we thank her.

I smile as I stir creamer into my coffee. The color reminds me of Cruz's skin. "He is beautiful. But it's more than that. He's just as beautiful on the inside as the outside." I sigh. "And good Lord, is that man beautiful!"

Grandma Clarabelle chuckles. "Yes, he certainly is." She looks at me and I notice the light in her eyes. "He did well today. He was scared, but he did well. This family is a lot to deal with. The stigma associated with him and his parentage is an old one. My stuck up son and his wife, your parents, are not going to approve of you being with a creole, a *mulatto*." She reaches over and covers my hand with her wrinkled one. "But then again, you're my grand-daughter. You are very much like me and you don't care what they think. You shouldn't."

I smile at her. She's right. I know people will disapprove of me being with Cruz, but the fact of the matter is that I don't care what others think. I care what I think. "I know and you're right. I don't care what anyone thinks. I only care what I think and what he thinks. And I think that I love that man. He's my future."

She chuckles again as she pats my hand. "For what it's worth, belle fleur... I approve very much of your choice."

My heart warms. Grandma Clarabelle is the only person whose opinion matters to me. "Thank you. It does matter. In fact, your opinion is one of the only ones that I give one hoot about!"

She squeezes my hand and cackles. "I know."

Leaning back, I close my eyes as I hold her hand and we stay that way until I hear her deep breaths, relaxed in slumber. I'm sure today was exhausting for her. She's not a spring chicken anymore. Getting up, I grab a throw from the fainting couch and place it over her as I kiss her forehead.

Heading across the hall, I check on Ty. He's snoring on the couch. I place a blanket over him as well and head toward the front of the house to find Cruz.

I check the front rooms and they're all empty, so I cross to the kitchen and let the housekeeper know Grandma Clarabelle is asleep in the parlor and she can head up. I'll wait around to help her to bed before we head out for the night.

Pouring myself a refill from the coffee pot before rinsing it and discarding the grounds, I head outside in search of my boyfriend.

I hear him on the phone and he sounds agitated.

"I will not! I have no desire to see him. I've told you that. I don't even understand why you want me to. I love you, Momma, but I'm not and you need to stop bringing it up."

He says a few more things and then he tells her goodnight. I don't want to seem like I was eavesdropping, so I make certain to make some noise as I open the door. His head whips around and I can see the pain and frustration in his eyes. My heart aches for him. I'm assuming that was about his "father" again.

Crossing the porch as he hangs up, I wrap my arms around his waist and hug him. He hugs me back. Tightly.

Chapter Nineteen

Cruz

I *don't know why Momma is so insistent that I meet with that asshole. I don't want to. There is nothing he can do or say that will make me forgive him for what he did. I'm not strong enough to do that. I refuse to. He's up to something and I am not going to be a pawn in whatever game he's playing.*

I hang up with Momma as I hear the front door open. Tifanie walks out and hugs me. I need the contact and I've never needed anyone other than my momma before. But, I need Tifanie.

Her arms wrap around my waist and I encircle her as she snuggles into my chest. She murmurs quietly, "Everything ok?"

I hug her tighter. "Yeah, fine. I had a missed call from my momma earlier so I just wanted to return it. She's on me about meeting with Lucian again."

I can see from her expression that she's confused. "Lucian? Wait... His name is Lucian?"

Her body feels tense, so I pull back to look at her. I nod. "Yeah, it is. Lucian Wormer."

She jerks out of my arms and throws her hands up over her mouth. The horror on her face scares the hell out of me. "What? You're telling me your father is Lucian Wormer?!"

"The man who raped my momma is Lucian Wormer, yes. How do you know who he is?"

She's unsteady on her feet and reaches out to steady herself before sinking into a chair. "Lucian Wormer was a friend of the family. I've never met him." She looks at me. "But, I've heard his name over the years. My parents knew him. He and my father both courted my mother and when she chose my father over him, he lost his mind. Grandma Clarabelle said that he struck my mother with a fireplace poker and tried to assault her..." She looks at me with an unreadable expression on her face. "My uncle came in and stopped it."

What did she say? The man who raped my momma attempted to do the same thing to *her* mother?!

I'm going to throw up. "What? Are you saying that the man who fathered me by raping my mother tried to rape *your* mother for choosing another man?!"

She nods. "Cruz... he's evil. You can't meet with him. I don't know what he wants with you, but you can't meet with him. People like that... Evil like that... It doesn't just go away."

How can I be involved with her now? Not only is she from an influential family, but my sperm donor attempted to harm her mother in the same way he succeeded in harming my own. No, no this can't happen. It was bad enough when it was just my momma, but with this new information, no...

I have to get out of here.

I stand quickly and it startles her. She jerks back in fright.

I did that. She just jumped because she was scared of me. I can't have her scared of me. I can't do this. I'm not meant to be with anyone. I have to go.

"I need to go. I'm going to call one of the guys to come get me. Go on back inside, Tifanie. I'm sorry."

She's staring at me with her mouth hanging open. She shakes her head in disbelief and stands up. I take a step back as she steps toward me. "What? What the hell do you mean you're leaving and you're calling one of the guys?!"

Taking my phone out of my pocket I press the button to call Dade. "It's best if I go. I'm not doing this to you. Go on inside."

She grabs my phone and hangs it up. I sputter, "What are you doing, Tifanie? Give me the phone!"

She shoves me and throws my phone off of the porch and into the yard. *What the hell?!* I'm so startled at the shove that I miss the second one as well. Then, she's in my face. "What the fuck are you doing? You're leaving now? *Why?!* What the hell are *you* doing?"

Holy shit, she's freaking pissed. Why is she pissed? I'm doing the right thing.

Why is she so mad? I'm doing the right thing. I'm doing what's best for her. I knew I wasn't good enough for her and now this... this proves it. I'm not meant to be with her. She's better than me.

Yes, I'm not the rapist, yet, I'm the one who has his blood. I care about Tifanie too much to stay and possibly hurt her at some point.

Walking away from her, I go down the steps and search for my phone in the grass. She follows close behind. I glare at her and she glares back. The fire in her eyes is almost scary. Yet, I hold my ground. "Stop yelling at me, Tifanie. This..." I point between the two of us. "This is not a good idea. Lucian is *evil.* You said it yourself. He's bad. His blood is in me. No matter what I say or do, he's a part of me. I came from him! Do you not fucking get that?! I don't want to be like him! I can't be like him! I cannot risk hurting you like that! Do you fucking understand that?!"

She's looking at me like I'm speaking Chinese. "*What?* That is the stupidest thing I've ever heard, you idiot! I *know* you aren't like him! You're nothing like him. Yes, he's evil personified, but you are *not! How the fuck are you so smart and so fucking stupid at the same time?!*"

She marches over to me and shoves me in the chest again before screaming at me. "I love you." My mouth hits the ground. "*Yes, I love you!* If you were evil, Cruz Edwards, then I wouldn't love you. I couldn't love you. But I do. I love you and now you know. I love you and even though you may not love me back, I love you enough not to let you throw this away." Her hands run over my arms and link with my fingers. "I love you enough that I'm not letting you do this. You're not running away from this. You're better than this. You deserve this." She whispers, "I'll love you enough for the both of us if that's what it takes!"

Her chest is rapidly rising and falling and her eyes are glassy with unshed tears. Once again, she's willing to fight for me. She keeps fighting for me.

The ringing of my phone makes both of us jump. Looking down at the grass, we can see the screen light up. Tifanie marches over and grabs it before holding it out to me. I see it's Dade. Still staring at the fierce and determined woman in front of me, I take it and answer, "Yeah."

"Hey, you called me and when I answered you hung up. You good? Did you need something?"

"I did call you. It was an accident." She's watching my face. "Sorry, man. I'm good. I don't need anything. I have what I need."

"Ok, cool. Later."

Before I can say "Later," he's hung up. Tifanie just stares at me and I stare back.

Tifanie just told me she loves me. I already knew she did, or I thought she did, but she said it. No, she screamed it. She loves me and she's willing to fight for me. I don't know if I love her. I think I might, but I don't know and until I do know, I'm not saying it.

But she loves me and she makes me feel. She makes me happy. I have to stop pushing her away and trying to ruin this.

She loves me and I want to stick around…

Are you man enough to actually do it though?!

Yeah, I am. I have to be.

She's searching my face and waiting for me to speak. What do I say?

Finally, I pull her onto the steps of the mansion and we sit down. She stares straight ahead with her hands clasped and her mouth tight.

I lean back on the step behind me and cross my ankles. Watching the moon, I say, "I'm sorry."

Her head turns and she looks at me. She still looks pissed. "You can't keep doing this." She glares. "You can't turn tail and try to run every time something scary comes along, Cruz. You're an adult. This is an adult relationship. It's not easy. It's not supposed to be easy. But you can't keep doing this."

I nod. "I know. But it's what I do. It's what I know how to do. When things are tough or get complicated, I leave. It's worked for me in the past. It's all I know."

She grabs my knee and squeezes. "It stops now. You're not running from me... from this." I cover her hand with mine. "I don't need everything, Cruz. But I need something. You have to give me something."

Leaning down, I stare into her eyes and slowly and shyly smile. "I know. I don't have a lot to offer. I have no idea what I'm doing, but I can give you something… I can give you me. I can give you me, Tifanie." Brushing her mouth with mine, I feel her sigh and then she smiles against my lips.

"Well, since that's exactly what I want… I'll take it."

The door opens behind us and I mutter, "Deal." I brush her lips with mine, before I turn to see who's come out.

Ty is standing there. His hands are shoved into his pockets and his feet are bare. His hair is rumpled and he looks embarrassed. "Hey, guys. Sorry to interrupt your moment here, but I just woke up. I think I drank too much."

I nod. "You had a lot. It's cool though. I think we're good here."

Holding out my hand as I stand up, Tifanie places hers in mine and I help her up. She smiles at me. "Yeah, we're good here." She lightly squeezes.

She turns her head to Ty and says, "You ok?"

He grimaces and nods. "Yeah, I'm good. Long day."

Nodding, she lets go of my hand as she heads up the steps and into the house. "I'm going to check on Grandma Clarabelle. If she's still asleep, I'll help her to bed and we can head out."

I nod as the door closes behind her and it's just me and Ty on the porch of a humongous mansion that neither of us belongs at. I chuckle at the absurdity of the situation.

Ty plops into one of the cypress gliders as I sit back on the steps and lean against the handrail.

After a minute, he breaks the silence. "So, where did you two disappear to earlier this afternoon?"

I smile as I remember where we went… and what we did when we got there.

"Oh, Tifanie just took me on a tour of the grounds."

He nods. "It's gorgeous, huh?"

"It is. This place is unbelievable."

The creak of the glider and the hum of the night sounds

are weirdly soothing out here. "Yeah. Hard to believe that Tifanie grew up here. She's nothing like the rest of them. I still can't believe she came from these people. Talk about the fruit falling far from the tree." His voice sounds pessimistic.

"Yeah. She's different for sure."

He's quiet for a minute. "I heard some of that." I look at him with a question on my face. *Heard what? How much did he hear?* He shrugs sheepishly. "I wasn't listening on purpose. But when I walked up, I heard some of your conversation. With Tifanie. Sorry, I know that was private."

I nod. "It's ok." Do I tell him that we heard him and Tifanie's sister in the maze earlier today? But what did we really hear? I decide to keep my mouth shut. I've never been one to get in everyone's business before. I'm not starting now.

He sighs. "So, you were trying to bolt?"

I chuckle. "Yeah, I was. I got spooked by something and I tried to get away from it. It's what I do. It's what I've always done. Only, Tifanie wouldn't let me."

He mutters, "Yeah, she's the one who fights for what she wants."

Nodding, I agree with him. She is a fighter. And an excellent lover.

Chapter Twenty

Tifanie

The house is quiet with everyone out and I follow the sound of Grandma Clarabelle's soothing snoring to the parlor. Gently shaking her, I speak quietly. "Grandma, let's get you to bed. Grandma, wake up. It's late."

I laugh as I realize I'm trying to wake up my grandma to get her to go to bed.

She opens her eyes and mutters, "Are you still here, belle fleur?"

Smiling, I fold the throw and place it back over the fainting couch. "I am. But it's late, so let's get you up to bed."

Her eyes crack open again and she smiles at me. Her eyes are twinkling from sleepiness and mirth. "So, you showed

Cruz your secret spot today?"

The blood rushes to my cheeks. I laugh as I help her up. "Grandma! How do you know that?"

Her hand cups my arm. "Cher, I know a lot of things." She chuckles. "I all but told you to take him to your 'Secret Garden.' He needed a break and it's a good place to think, talk, and… relieve some stress. Why do you think I sent you that way?"

"Grandma!"

"What, cher? I'm old, not dead. And you two were gone for over an hour. You also had flower petals in your hair when you came back and a… glow."

Oh my God… Grandma is telling me that she knows I took Cruz to my Secret Garden and had my way with him today. She's hilarious. I'm embarrassed, but not as much as I probably should be. I never knew she knew about my secret place.

I chuckle as I help her steady herself on her feet. "Yes, well…"

She pats my arm and I look over to see her with a dreamy

expression on her face. "Passion is important in a relation-ship. Love, trust, and passion. Those are key. Relationships are possible without love. Some are possible without passion, but for a truly life-changing relationship that will span the ages and soothe the soul, you need all three." She's talking to me, but it also seems as if she's talking to herself. Her face turns toward me as we reach the landing on the grand staircase. "You have all three with him, cher. That's something special and you need to hold onto it. Don't let other people take it away from you. You are strong and stubborn. Stay that way. Don't let anyone sway you."

My mind is racing. What is she talking about? "Grandma? Did you love someone who got away?"

She smiles sadly at me. "I loved someone. But he didn't get away. I let others make him go. It was much different in those days." She pats my hand again and sighs. "It's a different time and you're a stronger woman than I am. If that man is what you want, then that man is what you need to have." She pats my cheek. "Keep fighting."

Wow, I never knew that.

I help her get into bed and tuck her in, the same way she used to tuck me in as a child, before locking up and letting myself out of the house. Cruz and Ty are waiting for me on the porch. It's been a long day, so we drop Ty off and head back to my place. We have to work tomorrow night, so he needs to rest up and get that alcohol out of his system.

Cruz decides to stay the night and we're both so drained from the day, we fall asleep almost as soon as we get into my house.

I've been at work about an hour and Ty has been unusually quiet. He's not his usual carefree, chatty self. I tried to ask him about it once, but he basically snapped my head off; I retreated to the couch with my Kindle to read while we wait for a call.

I'm absorbed in the Gabbie Duran book I'm reading when I see Ty stop in front of me. I look up with a question on my face. He smiles sheepishly. "Sorry. I'm a bear today. I'm in a pissy mood and I'm taking it out on you."

"It's cool. Everyone has days like that. You ok?"

He nods. "Yeah, I let something get to me and I know better. I'm good." He waggles his brows at me and smirks. "So... I hear that Cruz tried to run last night and you put him in his place."

I laugh. "You heard that, huh?"

His face sobers. "Yeah, I heard y'all. I wasn't eavesdropping, but when I got to the door, y'all were arguing. I couldn't interrupt, so I let you finish."

I sigh. "Yeah. I told him I loved him in my rage."

His head whips around. "The fuck you say? You told him what?!"

I laugh. "You heard me. I told him I loved him. I was pissed and it came out. He was shocked. His face was kind of priceless. But it was good. We're good. I think."

"Wow... ok then. I mean I'm not surprised you love him. I've known that forever, but I'm surprised you told him.

Though, I guess I'm not really that surprised about that either. You do tend to go after what you want. It's one of your more endearing traits." He bumps my shoulder with his.

"Yeah, I to tend to go in guns blazing."

He murmurs, "That's not always a bad thing. At least you know what you want and you go for it."

I nod. "Yeah, I know what I want." Turning to him, I grin. "And I think I have it now."

He chuckles. "That man never stood a chance."

I hope he's right. Deciding to approach what we heard last night, I ask, "Ty? Cruz and I were in the maze." He looks at me and he frowns. "We heard you. We heard you arguing with AnnaBeth... What was that about?"

He laughs harshly, "You know me. And you know I can't stand her."

I nod. "Yeah, but it seemed like more. Are you sure that's all it was? You would tell me if something was going on, right?!"

He looks at me and smiles. "Trust me, Tif, nothing is going on. I would tell you." He laughs. "Me and Anna-Beth..." He shudders.

I chuckle with him, of course nothing is going on with them. They hate each other.

We get a call. *"Altercation at a private residence. Two males, one female. Neighbor called it in. At least one appears to be wounded. Not certain of the extent of the injuries."*

Ty grabs the keys to the "bus" he usually drives, and we head out to the location they give us. We chat about nothing on the way as Ty navigates through the light traffic with the lights on. It's a nice neighborhood near the Country Club. I can't help thinking to myself it's a strange location for an assault call like this.

Ty parks behind the police already on the scene and we grab our bags as we head up the drive to see what we're dealing with.

As we round the corner of the drive, my heart drops as I scan the crowd. Cruz is here. Why is Cruz here?

Ty recognizes him as well and he shoots me a questioning look. *What the hell is this?* There's no time to think too hard about this as I try to focus on the situation. A friend of mine, Willis, is the officer at the scene. He walks out to talk to us as his partner talks to Cruz. I'm concentrating on the details he's providing when I notice a beautiful, black woman on the steps of the house. She's talking to another officer and gesturing to a parked police car. A man is in the back.

Cruz turns and I can clearly see his face for the first time since we arrived. *What the fuck happened to his face? Is he the assault victim? What the fuck is going on?*

Keep it together, Tifanie. You can't go all crazy concerned lover right now. Right this second, you're just a paramedic and he's just a patient. You can figure it out later, but right now, dear God… right now, hold your shit together.

Ty masks his face as he looks from me to Cruz. He leans down. "I'm taking lead. You assist. You can't be unprofessional right now. I know you know that and I know you're wanting answers, but they're going to have to wait."

I stiffly nod in agreement.

Ty nods at Willis and his partner, Shelton. Shelton says, "This is Robert Edwards. This is his mother's home. A neighbor called us when they heard shouting from inside followed by a large crash. He was attacked with a chair and has some minute lacerations on his face and hands from fighting off the attacker. His right bicep has a deep laceration with substantial bleeding that may need stitches. He was also clocked in the head so he has a possible concussion."

Ty smiles slightly. "That hard head will be fine."

Cruz grimaces as he stares at me. "It is hard," he says. "It hurts like a bitch, too. He threw my momma's antique brass lamp at me and it hit me square in the back of the head."

I take the blood pressure cuff out and start taking his vitals and Ty leads Willis and Shelton a bit away. They are talking quietly.

I need to remember to thank him later.

"So, what happened?" I keep working as I ask.

He frowns as he grimaces as if in extreme pain. "Momma called me when he just showed up. He said since I wouldn't meet with him, that he was going to come here so I wouldn't have a choice."

My hand tightens on his arm and his breath hisses out. "I'm sorry. I'll look at that in one second. I just need to grab some gauze to wrap it."

He nods. "Ok. I raced over here and told him to get out. He laughed at me and said he wasn't going anywhere. He said I was his son and he had a right to know me. We got into it and I told him again to get out before he really pissed me off. It got really heated and when I tried to throw him out, he grabbed the lamp and hit me with it. Then, he grabbed a chair and broke it over me as he hit me with it. He also stabbed me in the fucking arm! I finally managed to get up and screamed at Momma to get out and call the police. She ran out and I restrained him. They showed up a few minutes later."

My lips are tight as I listen to the hell he endured today. I knew Lucian was bad news. Cruz was right to want to avoid him, but if he just showed up here, then he's stupider than I originally thought.

Of course he also raped Cruz's mother twenty-six years ago, so I can't imagine what he's thinking right now.

After cutting away the sleeve of Cruz's long sleeve shirt, I check the wound on his bicep. I mutter a curse. "This needs stitches, Cruz. No major damage, but he cut pretty deep and your tattoo is going to be fucked up with a scar."

He mutters a curse, too. "Shit! Can you stitch me up?"

I look up sharply. "I'm not a doctor, Cruz."

"I know, but you can stitch me up, right?"

I look at him calmly. "I can, but I also have to check for wood splinters. It's going to hurt."

He nods. "Ok, then do it. I trust you and I don't particularly care for hospitals."

Ty, Willis, and Shelton walk back over. Willis flips his pad closed. "We have everything we need for your statement. We're taking him in to the station to be booked. But, be forewarned, he won't stay there. Even with the litany of charges, with his name and all… I wouldn't be surprised if he's out by morning… even with the parole violation. My advice, like I told your mom, get a restraining order."

Cruz nods. "Thank you. We will. We both will."

They watch as I probe the last of the gash for splinters. His breath hisses out as I finish and stitch him up. When I'm done, I wrap his arm.

We're left alone again as Ty walks with them, talking quietly. I can see them all casting covert glances at us.

Cruz notices too. "Great, let the tongue wagging begin."

I laugh lightly. "Yup, best way to have gossip make the rounds is tell some cops."

He rolls his eyes. "Yay, me. Sorry."

I ask with surprise as I clean and bandage the rest of his injuries, "Sorry for what?"

He laughs. "For being the subject of more speculation and gossip thanks to me."

I grin at him. "It's ok. You keep life interesting." He

laughs with me before cussing as I bandage a particularly nasty cut above his eye.

We're interrupted by a soft voice. "I'm assuming this is Tifanie?"

Chapter Twenty-One

Cruz

I'm sitting here in my momma's driveway surrounded by cops with Lucian in the backseat in handcuffs as Tifanie sews up a deep cut on my arm. That asshole broke a chair over my back and then stabbed me with it in my arm.

Thank God he came after me and ignored Momma. I was able to engage him enough to get her out of the house and call the police. She's safe. If he'd tried to hurt her again, he'd be leaving in a body bag and not a cop car.

He did a number on me, but only because he snuck up on me. It was stupid of me to turn my back to him though. My vision is spotty and I feel like I'm going to hurl, so I'm pretty certain I have a concussion, not to mention the cut on my arm and my face feels swollen too. I got him too, though. Once I was able to get up, I gave him a pretty good lashing before I restrained him.

I was hoping it would be anyone but Tif and Ty to show up here, but I'm kind of glad it was them now. I don't want to go to the hospital and I'm comfortable with her stitching up my arm, though it hurts like hell.

She mutters a curse and I look down at her. Her face is scrunched up in concentration and she's biting the tip of her tongue. She tells me that the cut is deep and went through my tattoo, meaning the scar is going to mar it. I cuss in rage. That tattoo is for Momma! And that criminal just messed it up.

But at least he didn't hurt her. That is the most important thing. He's also under arrest for breaking and entering, kidnapping, assault, and his parole violation.

The cops walk back over with Ty and tell me Lucian will more than likely be out by morning. It infuriates me, though I already figured as much since he's a rich asshole with a powerful family behind him. They say Momma and I both need restraining orders.

Oh, she's getting one. This is one thing I am going to make her listen to me about. She's getting a restraining order.

As the officers walk off with Ty and whisper about me and Tifanie, I glance over at Momma. She is pale and wringing her hands as she watches a cop car leave her driveway. I make a smartass comment under my breath about the gossiping that I'm certain is happening.

Tifanie laughs and replies about cops and rumors.

I don't like it. I don't like that people are going to talk about her because of me. I don't care if they want to talk about me, but they are not going to talk about her. They shouldn't talk about her.

As she's smirking and grinning and being Tifanie, I'm thinking about all the shit that they could be saying and getting angry and annoyed making my head hurt worse than it already does.

What a shit day!

Suddenly, my momma is next to us. I never heard her walk over, but here she is… asking, "I'm assuming this is Tifanie?"

Tifanie looks at me quickly and then smiles up at Momma. She stands up and takes off her gloves before holding out her hand. "Hello, Ma'am. You would be correct. I am Tifanie. And since he looks just like you, I'm guessing you're Cruz's beautiful mother."

Momma looks Tifanie over in her pressed uniform and pulled back hair. She smiles and takes her hand in a gentle shake. "Hello. I'm Corrin Edwards, his mother, though I'm not sure of the beautiful part. Thank you for taking care of my baby."

Tifanie grimaces. "Well, it is my job. Though, a heads-up that he was my call might have been nice."

I sputter, "Yeah, because I totally freaking planned this shit."

Momma glares at me. "Robert Cruz Edwards, you watch

your tone. Tifanie just sewed up your arm. No one planned this. And I imagine she was saying she was shocked!" She mutters under her breath about manners. "I would think seeing you here was unexpected."

I feel chagrined. I'm almost twenty-six years old and I just got scolded by my momma… in front of my girlfriend. *Wait, my girlfriend? Did we determine she's my girlfriend? Why would she want to be especially after today's events on top of past events? Why the hell is she not running like Flo Jo?!*

Tifanie smiles and my insides ignite. I stand up and almost fall on my face. Fucking concussion.

Momma and Tifanie both grab me before I hit the ground. Tifanie calls out, "Ty! Help us! This stubborn ass has a concussion."

He runs over after closing the back of the ambulance and takes me from my momma with his arm around my waist as they lead me toward the house. As we get to the front door, I take in the destruction on the inside and groan. What a mess!

Momma's face is pinched as she looks around. There's blood on the carpet where Lucian and I scuffled, though to be honest, I'm not certain of whose it is. Tif frowns.

She looks at Ty. "I'm going to need the rest of the shift off."

He nods. "I know. I already called it in and said you had a personal emergency. Bently is coming in to work with me."

I see her nod and hug him before I close my eyes. I hear, "Thank you, Ty. I'm going to stay here and help clean up. I also want to keep an eye on Cruz with that bump on his head. Stubborn ass!"

I squint at them. "I can hear you, you know!"

She glares at me. "I'm aware!"

I see Momma smirk as she walks to the couch. She fluffs a pillow and places a blanket over me. Tif sits next to me. "You can go to sleep, ok? You have a concussion and since you won't go to the hospital, you can go to sleep, but I'll need to wake you frequently, ok?"

I nod and the movement makes me want to vomit. I just

want to rest.

She rubs my leg. "Go on and go to sleep. I'll stay here and check on you. I'll also dim the lights. Do you feel like you need to vomit?"

She's so stubborn. I know she's a paramedic, but the thought of her wanting to stay here, to take care of me… it makes me feel all warm and fuzzy. Maybe it's just the trauma to my brain though. I murmur, "Yeah, I'm really nauseated." She gets up, but it's way too much effort to open my eyes to see where she's going. I just want her to come back though.

I feel her set something next to me on the floor and her cool hand touches my forehead. "I put a trash can next to you. If you need to puke, it's right there."

Momma says quietly, "I'm going to make some tea. Would you like some, Tifanie?"

I crack my eyes open and look toward my feet. Tifanie nods at my momma and says very quietly, "I would love some. Thank you, Ms. Edwards."

Momma glances from me, lying on the couch, to Tifanie,

sitting at my feet and smiles softly. "It's no problem, sweetie. And please, call me Corrin. You are, after all, with my stubborn son."

My eyes fly fully open and I groan as my head complains heartily. I mutter, "Hey, be nice to the dude who got hit in the head. And stabbed!"

Closing my eyes again, I hear her soft footsteps disappear into the kitchen. Tifanie scoots closer to me and moves to the floor near my hip. Her hands are rubbing my head softly and with the soothing gesture and her whispered voice, I drift into slumber.

I can't be awake. I just went to sleep… But I am awake. Something woke me. What is it? Some whisper of a sound in another room woke me. What is it? What time is it?

Opening my eyes, I see that I'm in my childhood bedroom. What am I doing here? We haven't lived here for fifteen years.

It's a small house, but Momma always keeps it neat. It's little, but it's homey. We're comfortable here. Momma works hard to keep us in this house. We always have enough food and I always get little trinkets and treasures when I'm a good boy. I try to be a good boy, but kids are mean. I don't talk to anyone. I keep to myself. I'm different and I get teased a lot.

My eyes are really light blue and my skin is light brown. I'm not white and I'm not black. Kids call me a zebra. I don't like it, but I just stay quiet and walk away and hope that they'll leave me alone. They don't though.

There's a girl in my class. She's small and really skinny. She gets picked on too, but she doesn't just take it. She's sassy, but she's nice to me because she's like me. Her brother takes care of her and she doesn't have any parents. Her name is Clove. She's kind of pretty. She talks to me and shares her snacks. I always have a snack, but I don't really like Froot Loops and I get them almost every day. She usually has an apple or carrot sticks. I like those better, so we share.

Today at school a boy pushed her down at recess because he said I'm her boyfriend and he called me a zebra. I don't like being called that. It makes me mad when people say it. Momma says people say that when they don't understand something. She says they are kids and don't know any better because they weren't taught the right way. She said I'm *perfect and her blessing, but it doesn't feel like that. I don't feel like a blessing.*

I hear her crying sometimes. I don't know why but I know something bad happened to her. I've heard things people say. I know people are mean to her… because of me.

It's not fair. She's a good momma. She takes care of me and loves me. She doesn't like when people call me names either. I don't tell her about what happens at school, but sometimes at the store or movies, people point and whisper and say mean things loudly enough that she can hear them.

I don't like when Momma is sad.

Oh, that's what I heard… Momma is crying. She has bad dreams. Sometimes, she wakes up screaming and crying, but when I go check on her, she's not really awake. She's just crying and fighting the bad man in her nightmares. The man who hurt her.

What is that? Is she talking? What is she saying?

I'm coming, Momma. I'm coming. I'm going to get big and strong and I'm going to stop the bad man from hurting you. I'm going to make the bad man never hurt you again.

I'm going to work really hard and I'm going to protect you from the bad man.

Don't cry, Momma. I'm coming. I'm going to take care of you.

Chapter Twenty-Two

Tifanie

I'm sitting on the floor in Cruz's mom's house while he's asleep on the couch with a concussion and surrounded by a hell of a mess. This is not how I expected my day to go.

I woke up this morning in a good mood. He was lying next to me after staying at my house last night.

I've been thinking about everything that happened this weekend, all day, and then I went to work. And the first call we got today was about him and the man who raped his mom and has been stalking him for a couple of months getting into a fight.

Not that I blame him for the fight. I can't believe Lucian had the audacity to show up here. But can I really say that?

Am I really that surprised about it all?

I know the family he comes from. I know how they operate. The restraining order is a good idea, but I'm going to make a call too. I'm a Bellaforte dammit. I might not use the name in my daily life, but I have it and I'm a part of that family. I can help them because of it and I'm going to use that. For the first time, I'm going to use that.

Ms. Edwards, no, I'm sorry, Corrin comes back in with two cups. She hands me one. "I didn't know how you took it, so there's nothing in it. There's honey, sugar, and Splenda on the counter in the kitchen though."

I smile. "I take it plain. I like my tea and coffee plain for the most part." I chuckle. "Well, I like the frou-frou coffees too, but I drink it plain most of the time."

She smiles softly as she gazes at Cruz, asleep on the couch. He's so big, he's hanging off of it, but he's knocked out. His concussion is going to drain him for a bit as his body tries to repair the brain trauma.

Her sigh breaks my concentration on Cruz and I look at

her. She smiles again and her face lights up. I can see the resemblance and I see that Cruz gets his good genes from her. She thanks me again.

I shrug. "It's not a big deal. Really. I want to be here."

"I know you do." Her eyes are centered on me and it almost feels like she's reading into my soul. "You love my baby."

Am I going to answer her truthfully? Of course I am. I do love him.

Nodding, I let my gaze trail over him. I'm so glad he's safe. Still looking at him, I answer her, "Yes, Ma'am. I do. Very much."

She chuckles. "I wasn't asking a question."

Her simple statement makes my head turn.

"I know you love him. Everything you've done for him the past few months... he talks about you a lot. More than he realizes... I don't think he knows what he gives away."

What? What does she mean? I can't imagine Cruz talking about me with anyone, even his mom. The confusion on my face makes her grimace.

"Ma'am?"

"No, he doesn't talk to me about you. He's a very private man as I'm sure you know. He says a lot with very few words."

I nod. I get that. He doesn't open himself up. He has this wall, not a wall, a damn fortress.

She continues as she looks away from Cruz and right at me. "It's what he doesn't say that tells me as plain as day that you are good for him. You love him and I love you for loving him. He deserves to be loved. He deserves to be loved by a quality woman who will understand him and give him his space when he needs it. He deserves someone who's willing to push him and not back down. He's a stubborn, strong man so he needs an even stronger woman." She smiles at me. "He has that now... in you."

I can't breathe. Cruz's mom is telling me the things I need to hear. My heart is racing and my throat is tight. "I do love him. I know that. I've known that for quite a while. I know I push him, but it's because I refuse to let him put himself down. I refuse to let him think he's not worthy... of anything. He's worthy of everything. He's an amazing man.

"You have an amazing son. Yes, he's gorgeous." Chills race up my spine as I think of his utter beauty. "But, it's so much more than that. He's just a good man. He loves his friends. He's loyal to a fault. He does for those he cares about without the first thought for himself. He's just amazing." My voice drifts off.

Corrin reaches out and takes my hand. Her hands have calluses, but are still soft. I look at her and feel slightly embarrassed at my declaration. Her face is lined with the force of her smile. "Some evil happened here today. In my home. I could be sitting here right now, shaking in the corner, about to crumble into a sobbing mess on the floor. But, I'm not. I'm here in the wake of that event with a beautiful woman who *loves* my baby as I've always prayed someone would love him. I'm here with you.

"You fight for my baby. You bulldozed his walls and I understand what a feat that was. You have a long and hard road ahead of you. Cruz is not an easy man. You can't tear down a lifetime of hurt and shame in a few months. Shame he never should have felt to begin with because he's done nothing wrong.

"God gave me that man. The way I got him I'll never understand, but I do believe that God has a plan and I know that everything that happens in our lives happens for a reason. Yes, I was raped by a terrible man, a man who showed up at my home today and hurt my son, but that rape gave me that beautiful boy." She glances at the couch before looking back at me and squeezing my hands. "His being attacked today and you showing up to be the one to care for him… I don't believe in coincidences.

"You are here for a reason, Tifanie. This room has two women in it who are willing to fight for that man.

"You fight for my baby. You make him see in himself what you see… what I've seen all along. You make him want to take a chance. He wants it. He needs it. He deserves it. So do you."

Tears are rolling down my face at her words. My chest is hurting from all of the emotion I'm holding in. His mom just not only gave me her blessing but told me that Cruz and I are meant to be together. I've been thinking that, but to have the mother of the man I love confirm it... there's nothing better than that. Well, other than him saying he loves me too.

Putting my mug down, I lean over and hug her. She stiffens for a minute and then her arms come around me as she hugs me back. She whispers in my ear, "You're going to make me beautiful grandbabies."

Leaning back, I grin at her. We're interrupted by Cruz moaning on the couch. He appears to be having a nightmare.

Corrin jumps up and starts rubbing his head. She looks at me in alarm. "He hasn't had a nightmare like this since he was a child. Damn Lucian for doing this to him!"

As she murmurs soothing words to him, I check his vitals. His blood pressure and heart rate are elevated. I decide to wake him.

"I'm going to wake him up. He might flail, so please back up. I don't want him to accidently hit you. It's probably going to take a bit for him to understand that he's here and not wherever he is in his mind."

Tears are making trails down her cheeks and she looks pale, but she nods to me and with one last caress to his head, she steps back.

Standing near his hip, I call his name as I gently tap his chest. I don't want him to jump and pop a stitch and I don't want to be catapulted across the room if his instincts kick in and he lashes out. "Cruz. Cruz, it's Tifanie. You're having a nightmare. I need you to wake up."

Nothing. I lean closer and start to carefully shake him. "Cruz, come on. It's time to wake up. It's just a nightmare. It's not real."

His moaning gets louder. I try harder. *"CRUZ. I need you to come out of this. It's a nightmare. It's not real. It's just a nightmare. Nothing in your mind can hurt you. Wake up. It's not real."*

He groans and flops back against the pillows as he gasps.

He mutters, "Sadly, that's not true."

Corrin leans over him and kisses his cheek. "Hey, baby. You're ok. We're all ok."

He grimaces. "We're not. You're not. Lucian is back."

She sits next to him and talks gently to him. I make a decision and leave them as I head outside to the porch to make a phone call.

Scrolling through my contacts, I find the number I need. Taking a deep breath, I press the button to make the call.

A crisp, no nonsense voice answers, "Senator Bellaforte's office."

This is happening. Speaking absolutely clearly, I reply, "Hello. This is Tifanie. Tifanie Bellaforte. The Senator's daughter. I need to speak with my father immediately. It's important."

The stunned silence on the other end makes me smile. She recovers quickly. "Yes, Miss Bellaforte. Just a moment. I'll put you right through."

Within twenty seconds, I hear my father's voice on the

other end of the phone. "Tifanie. Are you alright?"

I sigh. "I'm fine, Father. I'm not calling for me. I need a favor. A favor you can help me with."

I hear something hit his desk and roll before he's back on the phone. "You need a favor from me?"

I nod though he can't see me. "Yes. I do. Lucian Wormer is Cruz's father. He raped and beat his mother. He's out of prison and assaulted Cruz today in his mother's home. I need you to make certain the charges stick and that the restraining orders are swiftly put through. I need you to get the word out about what he did today. I need you to do this… for me."

I can hear him swallow. "Tifanie… you and Cruz…"

Leaning against the porch railing, I give it to him straight. "Yes Father. Me and Cruz. I love him. He's going to be in my life. Whatever happens down the road, he's going to be here. You can choose to accept it or not, but I love him. He's in my life. I'm asking you to help me make certain that the man who hurt his mother… who attempted to hurt mine, your wife, gets what's coming to him. I'm asking you to help me protect the man I love."

I don't hear anything. He doesn't speak. Everything is quiet and I'm wondering if he's going to answer me.

I hear a deep sigh. "Ok. I'll make the calls."

He will? "You will?!"

He lets out a surprised chuckle. "Yes, I will. You've never asked me for anything before. You make it a point not to ask us for anything. Everything you have and everything you do, is yours. You're my daughter and I love you, so if you love this man, then he is obviously someone worth getting to know. I'll make the calls."

Wow. Is he accepting that I love Cruz?! I'm speechless.

"Oh, and Tifanie?"

"Yes, Sir?"

"How about bringing him to the house for brunch on your next free Sunday. I'd like to sit down with him... and with you."

I smile. "Yes, Sir. I'll talk to him and let you know. Thank you."

He replies, "Do that," and hangs up.

Leaning my head against the railing, I take a deep, deep breath before I straighten and head back into the house.

Chapter Twenty-Three

Cruz

I wake up and look around at the mossy green walls of my momma's living room. I remember being woken up a lot last night... a lot. Tifanie stayed the night here to take care of me.

I try to sit up and my head protests, but it's bearable. Slowly turning my head, I look around. The mess is cleaned up and the blood is gone from the carpet. I smell coffee brewing.

As I try to stand, I hear a sleepy, "How are you feeling?"

Grinning down at her as she straightens in the chair, I reply, "Like I got hit with a chair and then stabbed." She has dark circles under her eyes, testifying to her restless night and her hair is flowing down her back as it circles her head. She looks beautiful.

She stands and grimaces as she pops her back.

Walking over to me, she looks into my eyes and says, "Any double vision?"

I smile as I look at her. "No, but then I could kiss two of you."

She pulls back with a look of shock and chuckles. "You're not kissing one of me. I need a toothbrush first. And damn, maybe I should have knocked you over the head a long time ago."

Rubbing my head where it's pounding, I smirk. "Not funny."

My momma pops her head out of the kitchen. "Good morning, baby. Your phone has been ringing for a bit. You might want to check it." She smiles at Tifanie. "Morning, Tifanie. I have coffee and fresh waffles."

I mutter, "Hey, dude with a brain injury. I don't get any waffles?!"

Both of my girls smile. My heart swells. I wasn't certain of how I'd feel with Tifanie and my momma being around each other, but they seem comfortable and my heart is strangely content.

With a little assistance, I get to the kitchen and we all indulge in waffles.

Four hours later, we're curled up on my couch since Tifanie is insisting on my taking it easy and my momma was saying she wanted to go in to work; she is an architect. Tif brought me home and is babying me while I alternate between dozing and rolling my eyes at the Twilight marathon she has going on my TV.

After three movies' worth of watching a shirtless teenager with a lot of muscles and a skinny white guy who appears to sparkle like diamonds in sunlight fight over a reasonably attractive white girl, I ask Tifanie, "What is the fascination with vampires anyway? Why is it sexy to bite people and drink their blood?"

She turns to me. "Really? It's not the vampires themselves, I don't think. I think it's more that they live forever, don't age... they're sheer perfection. Well, except for the fact that you have to drink blood to survive. It's what all humans want. And they have it, so it's something we're fascinated with."

I mutter, "I don't want to live forever."

She leans her head on my chest. "I don't either. But you have the looking perfect part down." She kisses my arm, above my stitches.

Sighing, I mutter, "I'm far from perfect, Tifanie."

Turning her head, she looks up at me. "I didn't say you were perfect. You're not. You are fatally flawed."

Well, damn. Tell me how you really feel. I'm fatally flawed. What the hell?!

I frown and she presses her finger to my lips. "Hush. You're flawed. You have demons. But we all do. You hold onto what happened to your mom as a crutch." I shake my head. "No, you do. It's your way of saying, 'No, stand back. Keep your distance. I'm not worthy.' But you are. What you fail to realize is that by pushing people away, by not accepting what's freely offered, you're not accomplishing anything.

"You are gorgeous. Like inhumanly gorgeous." I shake my head in denial. "You are. You know it, you can see it. Yet, you refuse to accept it. But as beautiful as your face is... and it's crazy beautiful, your heart is the most attractive thing about you. I love the face, don't get me wrong." She leans up and kisses the scruff on my chin. "The face is amazeballs. But the heart... the heart is what I'm after."

Wow... she knows how to make a point. I can't even understand why she's so interested in me. Maybe that's the problem though...

"Why?"

"Why what?"

"Why do you want me so badly?" I really want to know.

She looks at me and in all seriousness, she says as clearly as she can, "Because you deserve my love."

Grabbing her, I pull her over me and kiss her. I kiss her

with all of the things I can't say with words in it. I try to tell her with my kiss that her loving me makes me whole. It makes me want to be the best man I can be... for her... and for me.

The sound of a lock and the door opening barely registers as I consume Tifanie.

A soft voice is at the door. "Sorry, guys. Excuse us. I'm so sorry to interrupt."

Then a humored voice says, "You got cracked in the head and stabbed in the arm; your dick probably doesn't even work. Stop leading, Legs, on."

Tifanie pulls back from me and grins. "Your friends are here."

Laying my head against hers, I mutter, "Why are we friends again?"

She climbs off my lap and I look around her. I see Clove standing there holding the baby. Liam is holding the diaper bag and smirking at me while wiggling his brows. Jessie is just grinning like an idiot and Blue is glaring at him and calling him a moron, while Dade and Melonie are holding delicious smelling bags.

Dade holds one up. "We brought food."

Clove smiles at me and walks over. "And I brought little John to see his Parain Cruz." She leans down and kisses my forehead before she sits and nestles the baby in her arms. Liam sits on the back of the chair and stares at the sleeping infant and the woman he loves. He looks up. "You ok, man?"

I gaze at the picture they present and my heart swells with... want?! *No, no way. I've never wanted kids. Well, I've never thought I'd have kids. I'm not thinking about kids. Not my own kids... I'm freaked out enough that Liam and Clove asked me to be John's godfather. No way I'm thinking about kids!*

Jessie and Blue walk all the way into the room and my living room is suddenly bursting at the seams. Dade places the bags down on the coffee table and says he's going to the kitchen for plates and forks.

Within minutes, I'm surrounded by my family as they all

ask what happened and how Lucian got to me. Dade finally asks, "Why did he want to meet with you so badly anyway? What did he want?"

The thing that has me the most worried about everything that went down yesterday is that I *don't know* what he wanted. He never gave a purpose for wanting to see me so damn badly. I'm worried that we haven't seen the last of him. Thankfully, we did get the restraining orders and we were called first thing this morning that they already went through. That was insanely fast in my opinion. I thought it would take weeks.

Shrugging, I look around at the room. "I don't know what he wanted. He never said. I got there and he was in the room with Momma. She was nervous and I flipped. I started screaming at him and things escalated from there. Before I knew it, he'd grabbed the chair and hit me with it, then he stabbed me in the arm with the broken arm from it before I was able to get control. He never said what he wanted. I'm thinking it's not good, whatever it is. For him to flip out like that and immediately attack me... yeah, whatever he wants... it's not good."

Dade says quietly, "We have your back, man... whatever you need. There're two reasons for the visit. One... we wanted to see for ourselves that you were ok. And two... Bradi is on her way over here for damage control. TMZ already has this story and they're broadcasting it everywhere. We need to have a pow-wow to see how you want this handled." He looks at me sadly. "I'm sorry, man. Your business is everywhere and I hate that Corrin is about to be subjected to this shit."

FUCK!! I didn't even think about that. I'm famous. Bayou Stix is famous and I'm in Bayou Stix. I never thought about the repercussions of the fight yesterday. SHIT! I need to call my momma. She needs to know what's about to happen. Son of a bitch!

I want to jump up and rage, but I don't. I hold it in. A hand on my knee brings me back. Tifanie looks at me. "It's ok, Cruz. We'll figure it out. None of that was your fault. Lucian is the one who's going to get the fallout from this.

Not you. Not your mom. But why don't you go call her. I can go get her and bring her here if you want. It might be better to have her close until this blows over."

"Tifanie is right. You need to get your momma and keep her here. People are going to swarm her like vultures. We can work with this. We can spin it, but it might be best if she's here too." We turn and see Bradi and Micah at the door. She walks in with her tablet already out. "I'm already working on something, but let's get your momma here too so I can go over everything with everyone." She looks at Dade. "Jude and Lexi on the way?" He nods.

Shit! Jumping up, I leave them in the living room and go call my momma. I hear everyone talking animatedly as I walk out.

As I dial, I feel a hand on my back. Turning, I see Tifanie. "I'm sorry. I know this is the last thing you want. I'll help however I can."

I nod at her as the phone rings. I don't trust myself to speak right now.

Momma answers. "Hello?"

"Hey, Momma. It's me. I'm going to come get you. You need to pack a bag that will last like a week. The media has the story about Lucian and what happened yesterday. They are going to try to talk to you because of the band. Because of me."

"I know, sweet boy. The phone has been ringing off the hook since you left and there are people camped on the street. I couldn't get my car out of the garage to go to the office. You shouldn't come here though. They'll follow us."

I don't know what to do. I have to get her, but I can't risk having them follow me back here either.

"Ok, let me figure it out. I'll call you back. Close all the drapes and windows though and lock the doors. Pack your bag. I'll call you back in a minute."

I hang up and throw the phone against the wall! *"FUCK!"*

Tifanie picks up my phone and hands it to me. She says, "I'm on it. I'll take care of it. Head back into the living room with your friends. And don't get upset. It'll make your head worse." She leans up and kisses me lightly. "I'm on it. I'm not a Bellaforte for nothing."

What does she mean? She's going to involve her family to help?

Turning, we see Dade in the doorway watching us. "She's right. She can do things we can't. Let's let her get Corrin and we can brainstorm here about what to do." He claps me on the back. "It's going to be cool, man."

Nodding, I follow him as he leads me back into the room. The room filled with my friends. "Yeah."

I'm trying to convince myself to believe him.

Chapter Twenty-Four

Tifanie

I was able to call my father and borrow one of their cars so it wouldn't be anything anyone recognized. As I park my car at the mansion to pick it up, my mom meets me on the porch. She's wringing her hands together and there are tears in her eyes. "It's true? Lucian Wormer is Cruz's father? He raped and beat his mother and she got pregnant? And then he showed up yesterday and attacked Cruz? It's all true?"

I nod at her. "Yes, Mother. It's true. Cruz is a good man. His mother is an amazingly strong woman."

She reaches out and touches my hair. "Oh baby, I'm so sorry. We were horrible to him when he was here. You love him. You love him and we love you, so we are going to help you. Whatever you need, you just let us know. No woman should endure that. And now, they are parading her story all over the news… it's like reliving it over and over and over. That poor woman."

I've never seen my mother like this. Reaching out, I take her hands. "Thank you. I need to get over there and get her. She's there alone and I don't want someone to get into the house or make her feel threatened. I need to get her, as soon as possible."

She nods and hands me the keys. "Of course. You go. Be careful." She touches my face again. "You're so strong. So unlike me. It's always scared me that we're so different, but I'm so proud of you. I've always been proud of you. You be careful. Ok, go. Take the truck."

I nod. I'm a little choked up, but I can't dwell on that right now. Right now, getting to Corrin is my priority. I'll deal with my own family later. "I'll call y'all later. Once we get to Cruz's house. Thank you, Momma."

She nods and steps back as she lets a sob out. "Be careful." I race for the garage and get the truck. Gunning the engine, I take off with a wave at the porch.

It takes me a bit to get to Corrin's house. There's a lot of traffic and media on the street and surrounding her house. Seriously, why are they doing this? This seems extreme, but what the hell do I know?!

I decide to park on the street behind hers. I can see her house from here and I'm surprised no one else figured this out. Parking under a tree, I head across her neighbors' yards. I'm trespassing, but I'm not hurting anything, so I hope no one stops me.

Glancing around as I get to her yard, I see nothing, so I sprint to the door and knock on the back glass. A few minutes later I hear her footsteps approach the door. Quietly, so as not to draw attention back here, I say, "Corrin, open up. It's Tifanie."

I hear the locks unclick and she glances out as she opens the door. I slip in and we close it back and relock everything.

She takes a deep breath. "Dear lord, why are so many people out there? I'm not famous. I'm a nobody. This is crazy."

Walking through the house, I peek out the front window and see slews of reporters and news vans. It seems like total overkill to me too. "I have no idea. Cruz is famous, but not that damn famous. I think this is more about the Wormers than anything else."

She shudders. "Damn him straight to hell!"

I agree with her. "Are you ready to go? Where's your bag?"

She points to the table where she has a small suitcase and another small travel bag. Grabbing the suitcase, I mutter, "Ok, let me make sure it's clear and then we'll head to the truck. I'm parked on the next street, so we'll have to cross through some yards, but no one saw me that I could tell, so we should be able to get back undetected."

She nods, but her eyes are huge in her face and she looks terrified. Taking her hands, I try to calm her down some.

"Corrin, I know this is insane. It's scary and I'm not even certain what all is going on, but it'll all be ok. I believe that."

She nods and smiles determinedly. "You're right. Just another something we need to overcome. We'll be fine."

Squeezing her hand one more time, I open the back door. As I'm about to step out, it's roughly shoved in and hits me in the face. I scream out as I feel my nose crack and try to shove back against it, but I'm weakened from the impact. The door is pushed in and then a body is in front of us. "Well, well... look what we have here. This is better than expected. I thought Corrin would be the one to get me what I wanted, but now I have both of the women in my *son's* life. You just made this too easy."

Blood is pouring from my broken nose as I glare up at Lucian Wormer. "How did you get here?"

Corrin screams at him to get out and Lucian levels a gun at her. "Scream one more time and I will shoot you. Shut up, bitch. With the circus out front, I don't need my plan ruined."

My eyes are trying to focus on the gun in his hand as he points it at Cruz's mother. I'm struggling to stay upright. Lucian looks at me and grabs my arm as he yanks. "Damn, you look like shit. Such a shame to mar up that beautiful face." He runs the barrel of the gun over my cheek and I stand tall and glare at him, though my insides are shaking and I'm about to vomit from the concussion he just gave me. He's insane. Not just evil, but insane too. I have to stay in control. I have to keep a level head.

Saying nothing and fighting back the desire to pass out, I just glare at him. He grimaces. "Get a towel. That's a lot of blood."

He's right though. If I lose too much blood, I'll be severely weakened and I need to try to keep my strength and my wits about me if I'm going to get Corrin and myself out of this mess. It's bad enough I'm already wounded from the door.

Grabbing a dish towel off the counter, I hold it against my nose and tip my head back slightly while applying pressure. I don't want to tip my head too far because that will just allow the blood to run down my throat. I try to make eye contact with Corrin, but she's too focused on the gun. Lucian gestures to the living room. "Ladies first."

Finally, Corrin looks at me and I try to convey a message. *We're getting out of this. I don't know how and I don't know what he's planning, but we're getting out of this shit.* She seems to understand. She nods.

As we get to the living room, he points to the couch and tells both of us to sit down. We do and he smiles. It's eerie and it's filled with malice. His eyes, the color of Cruz's, are wild. As he walks around, he picks up photos placed around the room. Most are of Cruz or of Cruz and Corrin. He mutters as he walks. Finally he stops on one photo. He picks it up and studies it and then he turns it around so we can see. It's a photo of the guys from the band. They appear to be much younger, and are holding a piece of paper in their hands and all are smiling at the camera. Even Cruz.

Lucian says, "My son. I'm so, so very... proud of him."

Pointing at me, he says, "Take your phone out. We have to make a phone call."

Thinking fast, I make a show of searching my pockets. "I don't have it. I'm sorry, I think I left it in the truck."

It's in my sweatshirt pocket, but I'm not calling Cruz. Not until I know what I'm up against here. I need Lucian to tell me his plans. He grins at me and a chill skates down my spine. He sits down across from us and crosses his ankles as if he's at the country club. "Well let's see… I've been in prison for a long time." He looks me over and leers. "A very long time." I hold in a shudder. "While I was rotting there, with no visitors, no companionship, no nothing except my cold, sterile cell, I would hear all about this amazing new band. This huge and famous band that was sweeping the country. Imagine my surprise when I found out my *son* was in the band. Now, I knew I had a son." He looks straight at Corrin. "Yes, I'd been informed that I'd impregnated you, Corrin, in our night of fun and passion." She shrinks back on the couch and the urge to attack him for what he's doing to her is pressing against me, trying desperately to get out. "Where was I?" He smiles coldly and his eyes twinkle. "Oh yes, I played my part well. I always was a miraculous actor. My face makes people want to believe me. So, I played them. I played them all. I..." He finger quotes, "found Jesus and started mentoring other prisoners. I even got to give seminars to adolescents at high schools." My look of disgust must be adamant on my face. He laughs shrilly. "Yes, can you believe how gullible people are?!

"I was up for parole and I was such a model prisoner who'd turned my life around, they couldn't wait to let me out.

"Only, I had no business left. I lost it when I was convicted. I had no money. I used it to try to pay off lawyers and judges. No life waiting for me once I got out. My family cut all ties. They can't be associated with me. Their names can't be tarnished. Do you think any of those assholes care that I have nothing left?! But, wait... my son has lots of money. He exists because of me. He *owes* me some of that money.

"I was going to play the doting father card. Make him think I gave a shit about him. But no, he refused to meet with me. He refused to take my calls. I engaged you, Corrin. I thought he's such a pathetic, wounded, momma's boy that you could talk some sense into him. I put all my faith in you, but you let me down. *You FAILED me!*"

He jumps up and gets into her face as he screams at her. "He exists because of me. I wanted you. You should have been smart and just taken me up on my advances. I was *rich and* powerful and I wanted *YOU.* You should have been grateful for that! If you wouldn't have rejected me after leading me on, none of this ever would have happened. This is your fault!

"I'm *not* going back to prison. I don't belong there. I'm a Wormer! Why do you think I'm here right now?!" He's screaming and his voice is getting higher and higher. "No one can control me. Even after everything you did to me, everything you took from me... *I'm powerful!* I can't be touched. Look at you both… I'm in control here. I'm the man. I'm a god and *you will not* fail me again, Corrin. You should have just accepted your fate. You were meant to be mine!"

Corrin is shaking and crying on the couch as he berates her with his lunacy.

Oh my God. He's completely deranged. He really thinks it's her fault. He's a sociopath. Oh my God.

Corrin raises her head, straightens her back, and looks him square in the eyes. "I did not lead you on, Lucian. I *never* reciprocated your advances. I told you as plainly as I could that I was not interested in you. Yet, you were fixated on me. You convinced yourself that you could take what you wanted. You raped me! You raped me and beat me, Lucian. Yes, I got pregnant, but that sweet boy is nothing like you. He's my son. Mine. He owes you nothing. No one owes you a damn thing. You made a choice and you *still* fail to accept responsibility. You have no remorse for your actions.

"Twenty-five years in prison for your crimes and instead

of learning from them... Instead of accepting Jesus and changing your life... You decided to make a mockery of everything and commit more crimes.

A god? You're not a god... you're not even a man.

"My son is not the pathetic one, Lucian. *You are!*"

Lucian's hand whips out, "Bitch!" and he smacks Corrin in the head with the butt of the gun. She slumps to the side, unconscious with blood trickling down her temple.

Immediately, I jump up and check her pulse.

He jerks my arm... hard and pops it out of its socket. I scream out in unimaginable pain. Before I can catch my breath, he's in my face. "Shut up. You shut up, you dumb bitch. You see what she made me do! We're finding a phone and we're calling, Cruz. That disgraceful abomination is going to give me what he owes me."

My eyes are crossing from the pain in my shoulder, but I know I can't call Cruz. If I do, he'll come here. He'll come here and it will not end well for him. Lucian will kill him. I see that. I see it clearly. I can't allow that to happen.

Shaking my head, I smile at him. "Call him yourself, you pathetic fucker."

He screams in rage and jerks me forward by my dislocated arm. My phone falls out of my pocket and slides across the floor, stopping as it hits the coffee table leg. I watch it... then, pass out...

Chapter Twenty-Five

Cruz

Tifanie has been gone for hours. Even with her going across the river to get one of her family's cars, she should have been able to get back here with my momma by now.

I'm pacing and checking my phone every ten seconds to see if I've missed a phone call or text from either of them.

Jude and Lexi are at the house now too and Erik and Alec will be here as soon as they can close up Java and Sweeties.

It's dusk and as the sky darkens, my worry increases. I have a feeling in my gut. Something is wrong.

Jude claps me on the shoulder. "Sit down, man. You're

going to wear a hole in the floor. Pacing is not making time go any faster."

Turning, I follow him to the couch and sit down. I jump right back up and resume my pacing. "I can't sit down. Something is wrong. Why aren't they back yet?"

Bradi has her phone and is frantically scrolling through something on the screen. She yells out, "Turn on the news. Something is happening."

Jessie whips his head toward me and turns on the TV. We settle on a local station and everyone's jaw drops as the words "Breaking News" flashes in red across the screen.

A cute blonde reporter is standing in front of my momma's house and talking into the camera. "Wormer is believed to be in the home. He was released from prison six weeks ago for the brutal rape and assault of Corrin Edwards twenty-five years ago. That assault resulted in the conception of Bayou Stix drummer, Cruz Edwards. Yesterday, Wormer was arrested at this residence for attempted kidnapping, breaking and entering, assault, and parole violation. Cruz

Edwards was injured in the altercation. Both Corrin and Cruz Edwards were granted immediate restraining orders against Wormer first thing this morning. It is under investigation as to why Wormer is out on the streets tonight.

A truck belonging to Senator Bellaforte was found on the street behind Corrin Edwards' residence. It's reported that the daughter of Senator Bellaforte is romantically involved with Cruz Edwards. Stay tuned to our station for the latest news. We're on scene and will closely follow and report on the story."

I can't breathe. Lucian is at my momma's house?! With her and Tifanie? That's why they aren't back.

Dade jumps up and stares at me with horror on his face. It's mirrored on the expressions around the room. Clove has tears running down her face and is kissing the baby's head repeatedly.

Dade takes out his keys. "Come on. I'm taking you to Corrin's. Jude, you come too. The rest of you stay here and keep us updated on any information." He kisses Melonie and points at Liam. "Try to keep everyone calm here and if you hear anything at all… *Call me!*" He looks at Jessie as the phone starts ringing. "Jessie, you man the phone. Do *not* give out any info. In fact, take it off the hook."

Everyone hops into action and I mindlessly follow them out of the house and into Dade's Hummer. He looks over and mutters as he backs out of the driveway, "They're going to be ok. You need to call the cops though and see why you weren't informed of this shit. You need to call them *now*!"

Jude takes my phone out of my limp hand and dials the number before handing it back to me. As it rings, another call comes in on my cell. "Tifanie."

My breath catches as I race to answer it. "Tifanie. Are you ok? Where's my momma? Are y'all together? The news says Lucian has you both in the house!"

A cold chuckle comes across the line and I drop the phone. Jude grabs it and puts it on speaker. "Well, well, maybe the media is not as ignorant as we make them out to be. Sorry, son, Tifanie can't talk right now.

"This is your father and you are going to do something for me."

My palms are sweaty and my heart is palpitating. "What the fuck did you do to them? Let me talk to one of them. Right now."

He laughs again. "I think not. Besides, even if I wanted to let you talk to them, you can't. They're both... *napping*."

My blood goes cold and my head is light. I seriously can't breathe. "What did you do?"

"It's not about what I did. It's about what I'm going to do if you don't give me what I want. What you owe me. I need money. A lot of it. I have none thanks to your bitch of a mother and I need some. I need money to get out of here and you're going to give it to me. Either you pay up, or your mother and lover will both cease to exist. I'll kill them both. But first, I'll sample them. It's been a long time since I've sunk into the softness of a woman."

Oh my God... Focus, Cruz. You cannot freak the fuck out right now. Stay calm. My head drops back. I have money. I'll give it to him, but how does he think he's going to get out of that house?!

"Fine. Tell me exactly what you need. Don't touch either one of them. Don't touch them or you won't get a dime."

"I want ten million dollars. I know you have it. I want it and I want it by today. You're also going to help me get a clear passage out of here. I won't savor them both if you give me what I want."

"I can get you the money. I can't do the rest. I'm a rock star, not a magician. I don't have those kinds of connections, Lucian."

"You don't… but Tifanie's *family* does. You'll make it happen. Had you just stayed in your own pool none of this would be possible. Thanks for dreaming big and succeeding where I failed, *son*."

Jesus.

Before I can form a thought, he chuckles. "Oh, looks like one of them is waking up. I'll be in touch. My money and my transportation… you'll make it happen. On second thought... your girlfriend is so very lovely..."

He hangs up. I punch the dashboard and Dade and Jude both cuss in frustration. Dade looks at me with fear in his eyes. "Cruz, that man is insane. There's no way anyone is just going to let him walk out of there after all of this. He won't touch them. He will never have the chance to get that close. Not with both of them." He grips the steering wheel as we turn onto my momma's street... on two wheels.

Authorities and news crews are everywhere. How are we going to get to her house?!

A cop stops us and says we can't get through and we'll have to turn around due to a dangerous hostage situation. Dade explains that I'm Cruz Edwards and that it's my momma and girlfriend being held hostage. He gets on his radio and a detective soon walks over. He motions for the barricades to be moved and waves us through. As we park, he meets us at the truck. He asks if Lucian has made contact and with Jude and Dade's help, I go over the entire conversation in the Hummer.

The detective cusses as he listens and jots down notes. When we're done, he looks up. "Ok son, I'm going to need you to help us. I want you to call him back. Tell him you're getting the money and that you're working on the way out for him. I need you to keep him engaged as long as possible so we can glean as much information as we possibly can. We know he's in there with two hostages and we think he's in the front room, but we need as many details as we can get. We also need to know their statuses. Are they hurt? Has he harmed them? If we can, we need you to talk to at least one of them. Are you up for that?"

I nod. I'm up for anything if it gets them out of there alive.

He directs us to a black van and ushers us into the back. He tells Jude and Dade to be completely quiet and then hooks my phone up to a device so the team in the van can also hear the conversation. Once he's got headphones on and a pad at the ready, he asks, "Are you ready?"

"I'm ready." He motions for me to make the call. It rings

once and then Lucian answers, "Hello, son. Fancy you calling me here." He laughs.

"Lucian. I'll have the money shortly. It's a lot of money to round up in a short time. I'm also working on a way to get you out of there, but I need to talk to either Momma or Tifanie first. I need to know they're both alive."

"I don't think you're in a position to tell me to do a thing, Cruz."

I look at the detective and he motions for me to keep the conversation going. "No, I'm not. But I'm working with you. I'm doing what you want. I just need to know that both of the women in there are ok. I'm cooperating, Lucian. Give me this. I need to know."

He mutters and we can hear him drag something then a weak, "Cruz? Cruz, is that you?" comes over the line.

My heart is pounding out of my chest at her voice. "Hey, Tifanie. Yes, it's me. Working on getting you out of there. Are you and Momma ok?"

"We're both alive. He's…"

A loud clatter is heard and then a crash. We can hear Lucian's roar and Tifanie curses. Another crash is heard and then grunting. We don't know what's happening. All we hear is noise and the sound of someone being hit. Dear God, please let Tifanie and Momma be ok.

A painful groan comes over the line, along with a large weight hitting something and then silence.

What just happened?

I holler into the phone. "*Tifanie!* What's going on? What's happening? Dear God... *TIFANIE!!*"

A breathless curse and then heavy breathing is on the line. "I'm ok. Well, no, I'm probably not. But Lucian, yeah, not so much. His head is angled funny, but I can't get across the room to check for a pulse. Send them in. Send the team in. Corrin is hurt. We need assistance in here."

Before she's done talking, I'm racing across the street and through neighboring yards. Cops and SWAT are heavy on my heels, screaming at me to stay back and that a team has gone in through the back. I ignore them and race for the front door. When I get there, I don't stop to think, I just kick it in. Before I can enter, strong arms pull me back. Willis, the cop from yesterday that Tifanie knows, is there breathing hard with sweat dripping down his face. "Stop, man. I know you want to get in there, but stop. Let them go first. They're trained."

Shaking his arm off, I duck under it and shove him with a quick, "Sorry, man," and run into the house. *Fuck that. That's my family. I'm going in.*

As I enter the living room, my eyes scan the room. A paramedic has an oxygen mask on my momma and she has blood trickling down her cheek from a large knot and cut on her forehead. They're loading her onto a stretcher. More paramedics are hovering over someone on the ground. I gasp when I see her. Her arm is hanging at a weird angle and her face is busted up. There's blood everywhere and her face is black and blue. The paramedics are fighting with her to lie down, but she's refusing and trying to sit up. Finally one of them helps her and she almost falls over. He catches her.

"Tifanie, your arm is broken, your shoulder is dislocated, your freaking leg is at least fractured, blood is running freely out of your broken nose, and you have a concussion. You did all you could! You probably saved both of your lives, now sit your stubborn ass down!"

Oh my God. What did he do to them? She's hurt like that. Those are some serious injuries.

The rage is racing through my veins and I just want to kill him. I want to torture him for what he's put these two women who mean the most to me through. How could he do this to the women I love?!

Roaring, I cross the room to the other side, near the fireplace where a large crowd is gathered around someone on the ground. It has to be Lucian. *Get away from him! I'm going to kill him.*

As I approach, ready to strangle Lucian Wormer after I plan on beating him unconscious, I see them place the white sheet over his face as his blue eyes stare unseeingly at the popcorn on my momma's ceiling.

WHAT?! He's dead?

The detective looks up. "He's dead."

My eyes bug out and my mouth refuses to function. He's dead?! How can he be dead?

Responding to my silent question, he inclines his head to Tifanie who's being fastened onto a stretcher. "Miss Jeffries. She fought with him over the phone and apparently is a black belt. She hit him in the throat to halt his attack and then kicked him in the chest making him lose his balance and fly into the brick fireplace. He broke his neck on the mantle on impact."

What the fuck?! My momma and girlfriend are being loaded into ambulances after being held hostage and assaulted by my rapist sperm donor who is now dead on the floor of my momma's living room after my girlfriend fought with him.

My vision goes black as Dade and Jude race through the door, calling my name.

Chapter Twenty-Six

Tifanie

---

*T*wo weeks. He's been avoiding me for two weeks. My arm is in a sling, my leg is in a cast, I'm surly as a bear, and I want to see Cruz. But no, he's avoiding me. In fact, he changed his phone number and sent a message through Melonie that I shouldn't contact him and he wishes me well and a full recovery.

WHAT THE FUCK KIND OF BULLSHIT IS THAT?! I'm going to kill him. Of course I can't drive because of my damn, stupid injuries, but I'm going to kill him.

I'm so mad I could breathe fire and I want to kill him, but I miss him and I love him.

Today is the day. I'm tired of this. No more games. No more avoidances. Today is the day.

I'm going to kill Cruz Edwards today!

I take extra time getting ready. It takes me four times as long anyway with only having one hand and arm and it being my left and I'm right-handed, but I'm determined. Everything is going to be perfect today.

As I add my perfume, I send a text.

"Tif:

Today is the day. No risk, no reward. Today it goes down."

I get dressed and slip on my shoes and a reply comes through.

"Ty:

No white flags."

I chuckle. "No White Flags" is Steve Gleason's motto and Ty and I absolutely love him. He's so strong and inspirational. Thinking about everything he deals with on a daily basis makes me think… *Damn right, no white flags.*

Everything worth something costs something and it's not about the hand you're dealt, it's how you choose to play the cards.

And dammit, I'm taking the house tonight.

My "Team Gleason" shirt is my uniform for this mission.

Once I'm ready, I make my call. Melonie has been expecting it and she's been checking in on me, so she answers on the first ring. "Hey, babe. Ready?"

Smiling, I reply, "Hey, babe. Today. It's today. Can you come pick me up?"

I hear laughter and then she says, "On it. I'll bring you back here."

While I wait, I decide to listen to some music to pump myself up. Mel is blowing the horn in ten minutes and as I slowly navigate the steps on the porch, I see blue highlights on the second head in the car. Blue is with her. She gets out and helps me in before slipping into the backseat. Leaning forward, she smiles at me. "Hey, girl. Sorry to invite myself, but we were at Java and Sweeties and when I heard what was happening, I decided to tag along."

I smile back. "No worries. Is he there?"

Mel shakes her head as she turns around in the yard. "No, he's at home. He's becoming a hermit."

I mutter, "Not after today." They both laugh as we head back toward campus to ambush Dade. I ask, "Does Dade know what he's about to do, Mel?"

She chuckles. "Yes. I told him. He's down. Everyone is. We all want Cruz out of his funk."

Smiling, I think to myself, *Excellent.*

A spot is open right in front when we pull in and Mel whips in. It takes me a bit to get out of the car with my leg and crutch, but Blue gives me a hand. As we near the door, it opens and a grinning Jessie is there. "Hello, lovelies." He swoops out his arm and grabs Blue, pulling her into his chest. "Can I get your number, sexy?"

She slaps his chest and bites his chin before kissing him. "You're an idiot."

He laughs. "I love it when you call me names. It makes me want to throw you against a wall and have my wicked way with you." He looks at me and smiles. "Hey, Legs. How are you feeling?"

Hopping over the threshold, I smile at him. "I feel like a frog who tangled with a blender." He chuckles. "But, I'm good."

He leans down and kisses my forehead. It startles me. "I'm glad you're ok." He points at me. "Now... you fix Cruz!"

I laugh. "That is the plan. I hope we can fix each other."

We've been making our way to the table in the corner that is fully occupied with the band and entourage, minus one, Cruz Edwards. Everyone greets me. It's nice to feel the love. Now, I just want it from the man of the hour.

Liam jumps up and offers me his seat. He's in a chair and everyone else is on stools. I plop down and glare at my leg.

Dade asks, "So, when are we doing this, Tif?"

Everyone at the table is staring at me. I'm surrounded by Cruz's friends and family, the people he loves the most in the world, and they are all trying to help me, willing to help me, scale his walls once and for all.

I'm the center of attention. "As soon as you can bring me to his house."

Jessie laughs. "Can I come? I want to see that white flag." He points at my shirt. "Though, I thought you wanted our boy to surrender?!"

I laugh. "I do. But Steve Gleason takes nothing lying down. He doesn't give up. He fights and fights. I'll fight for Cruz too. He knows this. We'd gotten to a good place and then two weeks ago happened. He recoiled. I was admitted to the hospital and he freaked. He stopped calling. He won't take my calls. He changed his freaking number and told me to have a nice life!" I slap the table. They all jump. "He changed his number so I couldn't call. Like I'm just going to go the fuck away. I told him I loved him and I know he loves me, yet he freaked the fuck out and just left me high and dry.

"I'm not fading away into the night. I want him. He wants me. I'm going to fight for his ass and he's going to accept that. More than that, he's going to embrace it. He deserves me. I deserve him. He's the prize and I damn sure want it. I deserve this! So does he!"

As I look around after my impassioned speech, I see everyone grinning. The girls are misty eyed and the guys look impressed. Dade stands up and plants a kiss on Melonie. "Let's do this then. Come on, Tif. Time to get your man."

We head to the doors amongst the cheers and Jessie calls out, "Scale the walls and take the castle! If he acts like Cruz... kick him in the moat and hold the jewels hostage!"

Dade yells back, "You're an idiot!" and everyone laughs.

He helps me into the Hummer and starts the engine. As he backs out, he looks at me and smirks. "You know he's going to fight you."

I nod. "I know. But I fight back. And I fight to win."

As he navigates traffic, he mutters, "I knew I liked you."

Half an hour later, he pulls under the trees in Cruz's driveway. Music is pulsating from the garage which I know to be his gym. Dade says, "Are you going in there or are you going to wait in the house?"

Thinking about it, I decide the garage is my best option. He's in there. He can't leave if I block the door. Looking at Dade, I say, "The garage. But I need to get the music off and keep him from leaving once I do."

He laughs. "The stereo is by the door. I'll turn it off and you can stand guard. I'll stay out here and stop him if he tries to leave."

I smile. "Thanks, Dade."

He smiles back. "Anytime. You love him. You're good for him. He was happy. You make him happy. Now make him see that and fix my boy."

I wipe my palms on my pants and he gets the door. I can see Cruz in the mirrors along the walls as he works out furiously. He's lifting weights and I get mad as I wonder about his arm and wonder who took his stitches out. I don't want to spook him though and have him drop the weights.

Dade motions to me that he's getting the music. He steps in and flips the power button as I stand near the door. The quiet gets Cruz's attention and he turns. His face registers his shock at seeing me there.

Dade smirks at him and salutes and then the door closes behind him. It's just me and Cruz. His labored breath and my pulse are the only sounds in the room for a long time. My leg is starting to throb from being on it and my hand is going numb from gripping the crutch so tightly.

He grimaces and I catch the guilt flash across his face as he looks at me. "What are you doing here, Tifanie?"

Rolling my eyes, I sarcastically reply, "Oh, I was out for a stroll and thought I'd stop by."

He grits his teeth. "Did the changed number not alert you to the fact that I don't want to talk to you?"

That hurts. My chest is burning, yet I'm not leaving until I get what I want. "No, it hurt me and pissed me off though. In fact, if my arm wasn't broken, I'd punch you in that gorgeous face."

His head jerks up and his light eyes darken as his nostrils flare. "You came here to punch me in the face?"

Staring at him, I fidget and try to get comfortable. "No. I came here because I love you and because you're pissing me off. I came here because once again you got spooked and ran and instead of just pushing me away like you normally do, you changed your fucking phone number! I came here because you're a coward!"

That gets his attention. "What do you not understand about the fact that I'm not good for you, Tifanie?!" He's screaming at me. "Look at you! Look at what he did to you!"

Calmly, I stare at him. "I know what he did. I was there."

He's shaking in his rage. "Do you know what that was like? Do you have any idea what that was like for me?

"There was nothing I could do. Not for you or my momma.

"I was helpless at the mercy of a madman! The two people who were the most important to me and both of you were hurt. Because of me!"

I'm staring at him because I think he really believes that. He really believes that what happened was his fault. I ask in shock, "You mean that, don't you?"

He's incredulous. "Mean what exactly?"

Staring at him, I drop my crutch. He watches me as I stand on my feet and try to take a step. "Cruz, what happened... happened because of Lucian. Not because of you. Lucian assaulted you. Lucian took your momma and me hostage. Lucian hurt us. Lucian attacked me and when I defended myself, Lucian paid the ultimate price for his crimes. *LUCIAN* is responsible, no one but *LUCIAN*. None of that has anything to do with you. You cannot let *Lucian win.*

"I love you. I'm willing to fight for you. I'm going to fight for you. I'm going to stay on you like a damn stalker if I have to. I will come at you over and over. I will not give up on you and I will not allow you to give up on yourself. I will not stop until I wear you the fuck down and you understand that you deserve to be happy. You deserve to have a life free from the stigma and guilt over someone else's choices. I'm not just going to let you push me away because you're scared and ashamed. I love you. You know that."

He's just staring at me, saying nothing. I have no idea if I'm getting through to him. That's the scariest part of everything happening right now.

He takes a breath and looks away from me.

I call his name to get his attention. "Cruz. Look at me." He slowly turns. "You know how I feel. I have no problem telling you over and over, every day if I have to, but if you can look me in the eyes and honestly say one thing... I'll leave. I'll walk out the door, well, I'm hobbling right now, but I'll leave and this will be done. If you can't put the Cruz Edwards that runs from everyone and everything into the grave, right now... bury that fucker... then, I don't know what else to do.

"I need you to answer me one question? Don't think about it and don't lie. There is no wrong answer. Can you do that?"

He nods.

"Can you look at me right now and tell me you don't love

me?" I hold my breath. Everything hinges on this one answer. If he can tell me right now and admit to not just me, but himself that he loves me, I will fight for him until I take my last breath. If he says that he doesn't... if he's going to lie, then he's lost to me. I can't keep fighting a losing battle if he has no intention of ever being true to himself.

He stares. There's absolutely no sound in the room except our erratic breathing.

Finally, he mutters, "God help me. I can't tell you that. I can't lie to you. Yes. I love you."

Did he just say it? I don't know if he really just said that. Should I ask him again?!

His face registers his own surprise at his confession. Crossing the room he stands right in front of me, but doesn't touch me. I look up at him in fear and hope.

As he looks down, his eyes travel my length and stop on each area that is hurt. He reaches out and touches me whisper soft before letting his hands fall to his sides.

"Yes, I love you, but looking at you hurts me. Seeing you

hurt, hurts me. Not looking at you hurts me. Not touching you hurts me. The fear that you'll wake up one day and stop loving me, hurts me. My heart hurts when you're near from fear that you'll leave and it hurts when you aren't from fear that you'll stay gone. No matter what I do, now that you're in my life, I'm living on a precipice. One step in either direction has the power to change my life.

"I've had these walls up for so long, Tifanie. And here you are, since the day we met... tearing them down, with bare hands when needed, brick by brick. I can't handle you. I don't know how to take you. I want to hold you and I want to push you away.

"My head is screaming at me to lock the gate and my heart is beating down the door and screaming the exact opposite while tossing you the key.

"I'm just... lost. I'm lost with you. I'm lost without you. Do I push you away or hold on and never let go? I don't know which is the right choice. Wanting you seems selfish, but not having you is unbearable.

"Yet, at the end of the day, there's only one thing I can do…"

My breath is in my throat with all he's saying. I whisper, "What's that?"

Leaning down, he kisses me softly. As he pulls back he mutters, "Surrender. *You win*. I'm waving the white flag. I love you. You love me. For whatever insane reason… you love me. It took you to make me see that I can be and I deserve to be loved. Because of you… With you, I'm ready to succumb. I surrender."

Smiling against his mouth, I forget my injuries and launch myself at him. He catches me and my shoulder gets jarred. The pain is brief, but the love I feel for the man in my arms is forever.

Bayou Stix Series Epilogue

Five-year-old John races by me and jostles my legs. I chuckle as I steady him. "Whoa there, careful, buddy. You're going to run over someone if you don't slow down."

He grins up at me with blue teeth. "I sorry, Parain Cruz. Kassi is chasing me and she said she's going to shoot me with her Nerf gun."

Kassi is a four-year-old mini-Lexi with her long red curls and amber eyes. She looks like a little doll, but she gives the boys a run for their money most days. She's got her daddy completely wrapped around her finger though and he loves it. I see her tearing around the corner like hell on wheels and John shrieks and takes off. As he races past Clove, she says, "John Zachariah Christianson, what are you eating? Why is your mouth blue? Did you eat sugar?"

He calls out as he runs down the hall, "Unca Jessie gave it to me. He said I could have it."

Clove hollers at Jessie, "*JESSIE ADAMS*! Are you giving my son sugar? You know it makes him a little crazy person! That's it, he's going home with y'all tonight! You can deal with that crazy! It'll be good practice for those sleepless nights!"

Jessie ducks into the kitchen where everyone is hanging out and preparing the food for tonight. "Aw, why you gotta be so mean? He's a kid. He can have some candy every now and then. And yes, he *can* come home with us!"

Liam switches arms where he's holding their two-year-old Gordon and three-year-old Lizzy clings to his legs, begging him to pick her up. He ruffles her hair and looks at Jessie. "Ha, you just did it. You two get the tornado tonight." He grins and points at a very pregnant Blue. "Just you wait. All this crap you've done for five years to all of us is about to be upon you, two-fold! Blue, are you ready for *TWO more* of Jessie?!"

Jessie grins and shakes his head. "Nope, we have girls in here." He walks up to Blue and rests his chin on her head after kissing her. He cradles her very large stomach.

Liam says, "Even better! Girls that act just like you. I can't wait to see you start to lose that long hair!"

Blue and Clove laugh, as Blue says, "Don't hex me with the curse of mini-Jessies!"

Clove chuckles. "Too late. You chose to procreate with him. Poor you."

Lexi pushes a squirming baby into Jude's arms and shoos him out of the kitchen. "Y'all get out. Go rock J.J. You're crowding my kitchen and I need to finish this cake." She looks at all of the men in the room and twirls her finger. "All you men folk, grab a kid, and someone make sure to watch Addy. Y'all know she's quick! Go on! Go to the media room or the backyard! The women need a break and can help me get this food out before Micah and Bradi get here." Jude salutes her and blows her a kiss as everyone herds kids out of the kitchen. She points at me. "But not you, Cruz. You stay here with us. I need muscle to lift this thing."

I trade a glance with Tifanie, my wife of the past four years, and at the sleeping bundle in her arms. Gracie, our three-month-old, opens her eyes and blinks. Her eyes mirror mine, though she's the spitting image of her momma.

As if on cue, her little pink lips pucker and she lets out a throaty cry as she nuzzles Tifanie's chest. My momma hears the cry and pops into the kitchen with Russ, our three-year-old son in her arms. "What's wrong, my little darling? Are you hungry? Your momma can feed you and then Maw Maw gets her turn with you."

George, Dade and Clove's surrogate father, has his arm around my momma and is holding the hand of a dark-haired, green-eyed little girl. She looks at him and her little cherub cheeks showcase her dimples as she smiles. "Paw Paw George, can I have a cookie?"

He tweaks her nose and snags one off the counter. "Don't tell your momma I gave it to you!"

Melonie rolls her eyes and laughs. "Serina, stop getting

your Paw Paw in trouble." She points at George. "I'm watching you!"

Serina bats her eyes at her mother. Melonie laughs. "That doesn't work on me, you little diva. I'm immune to those dimples."

Dade walks into the kitchen with his hands full of wood from the back-yard. His two-year-old son, Paxton, is carrying twigs next to him. He catches the tail end of the conversation and swoops in to plant a quick kiss on Melonie's mouth. "You sure about that?"

She blushes and he winks. She mutters, "Yeah, well you don't count."

Erik snags a beer and swoops up Pierson, Bradi and Micah's three-year-old. He squeals and laughs as Erik tickles him. "Come on, champ. Let's go throw the ball outside. We can beat Uncle Alec and Uncle Jude in a game of football."

Finally, the kitchen is empty of kids. Lexi sighs and points to the fridge. "Grab a beer, Cruz." She looks around the mess in her kitchen and chuckles. "Ok, troops. I need veggies chopped, this cake iced, those brownies cut, the gumbo stirred, those eggs filled, and some peace and quiet."

Melonie heads to the gumbo pot. Clove attacks the pile of vegetables and starts furiously chopping. Lexi puts the brownies in front of Blue and tells her to cut, but not stand up. I stand there clueless as the women get into the meal. A bit later, I feel a hand glide over my back and a shudder runs through me. Turning, I see my beautiful wife. She leans against my back and I pull her around to hug her. "Gracie is tucked snuggly in your momma's arms and Russ is asleep on the couch with her and George."

I nod and kiss her softly. Who would have imagined that so much could happen in six years!?

Six years ago, Bayou Stix was a family made up of five guys from different backgrounds who made awesome music together and were loved by strangers around the world. Now, the five of us have wives and babies. Our small family has expanded exponentially and we couldn't be happier.

George and my momma have been seeing each other for

a few years now. They are a wonderful couple and they both eat up all of the grandkids, all of them. Paw and Verna have also been married and will be here shortly.

Between the five members of Bayou Stix, we have nine kids... add in Jessie's soon-to-be-here twins and Bradi and Micah's two, and there will soon be thirteen little people running around.

Career wise, we've had four more platinum records, four sold out tours, and endorsement deals in the millions. But none of that... none of that compares to what we have right here.

Family. Friends. Love... That's what's important.

I'm snapped out of my musings as Lexi looks up and squeals. "It's time! Everyone get back in here!" The kitchen is soon crowded as everyone piles back in. We all stare at the television as we wait.

It's taking a while, so I look around the room with my arm around Tifanie. Momma and George walk over. Gracie is asleep in my momma's arms. Russ is holding her hand, but switches to mine when he sees me. George is standing next to Momma and holding Paxton. Dade is hugging Mel as Serina clings to his legs, sucking her thumb. Erik and Alec are holding hands while both have one child belonging to Bradi and Micah in the other arm. Jude wraps his arms around Lexi after she takes the sleeping baby and the other two kids climb onto the bar stools around them. Liam is holding Lizzie and Clove is watching Gordon and John play at their feet. Jessie walks up behind Blue and cradles her stomach as he rests his chin on her head.

We all hold our breath. The results are flashed across the screen and we all whoop and holler. It wakes the babies and they start to cry.

We laugh as a commotion is heard at the door and we turn. Jude calls out, "Welcome and congrats, Congressman Stevens!" as a beaming Micah and a glowing Bradi waltz in and head straight to their kids.

Bradi leans down and everyone listens as she tells their drowsy fourteen-month-old, Tristan, "Daddy won, baby!

Your daddy is the newest Congressman in Louisiana!"

We all clap and look around at each other in the noise and chaos. Everyone hugs and high fives.

This is the life. This is what life is about...Love, friends, and family. It doesn't get any better than this.

Stay Tuned early 2015 for a brand new

TWO books series

featuring:

James Black

Letter from the Author

Wow, this book marks my sixth novel in a little more than fourteen months.

What an amazing fourteen months it's been. If someone had asked me in the beginning of 2013 what I saw for the next two years, I would never have imagined this would be my life.

I decided to write Alluring Turmoil on a whim one day last summer and I had no idea what I was doing. I sat down and just wrote... and wrote... and wrote. I poured my heart and soul into those pages and then I made a split second decision to roll with it and see where the dice would land. I researched and found an amazing Cover Designer, a brilliant formatter, a pretty fantastic editor, and made some friends. Most of these people are still with me today and the friendships and support I've received have been simply unimaginable.

Last year, I birthed an idea for a series of books called Bayou Stix... This year I'm an Internationally Bestselling Author with THAT series. I've attended events where people traveled to see me and talk to me about my books. I've communicated with people from all over the world and all walks of life who have found pleasure and entertainment in my words. I've formed friendships with people I once admired as I devoured THEIR written words. This is truly what it means to "live the dream."

Thank you to everyone who's fallen in love with my words and characters. Thank you to those who haven't and have slammed both me and my work, you motivate me. Thank you to those authors who have offered advice and support. Thank you to the less than a handful of authors who have blown me off; you've shown me what I NEVER want to be. I have absorbed everything and I'm a constant work in progress.

This book is the last of the Bayou Stix series... I've loved these characters and they will always have a place in my heart; they are my babies, but I have so much more to tell you. So much more to share and I just hope you follow along for the ride.

Let's leave the top down and see where the road takes us...

Thank you all and may we travel this winding road together. I'm excited to see where it leads!

Love y'all,

Skye Turner

Playlist

Meghan Trainor – All About That Bass

Shinedown – All I Ever Wanted

John Legend – All of Me

Maroon 5 – Animals

Juvenile – Back That Thang Up

Ne-Yo – Because Of You

Art Of Dying – Best I Can

Calvin Harris – Blame

Jason Aldean – Burnin' It Down

The Chee-Weez – Callin Baton Rouge

Gloriana – Can't Shake You

Kardinal Offishall – Dangerous

Evans Blue – Erase My Scars

Maroon 5 – Feelings

Pitbull – Fireball

Drake – Forever

R5 – Heart Made Up On You

LSU Tiger Marching Band – Hey Fightin' Tigers

Hunter Hayes – Invisible

Maroon 5 – It Was Always You

Nick Jonas – Jealous

Glee Cast – Loser Like Me (Glee Cast Version)

Hoobastank – Magnolia

Katy Perry – Not Like The Movies

Imagine Dragons – Nothing Left To Say / Rocks

Spank the Monkey – One and Only One

Chase Rice – Ready Set Roll

Luke Bryan – Roller Coaster

Shinedown – Save Me

Nickelback – Savin' Me

A Great Big World – Say Something

Journey – Separate Ways (Worlds Apart)

Taylor Swift – Shake It Off

Escape the Fate – Something

Lifehouse – Storm

Hoobastank – The Reason

Madison Rising – The Star Spangled Banner

Colbie Caillat – Try

Muse – Undisclosed Desires

Linkin Park – Until It's Gone

10 Years – Waking Up

Tyler Farr – Whiskey in My Water

Chris Young – Who I Am With You

About the Author

Skye Turner

Skye Turner is an avid reader and an editor turned Internationally Bestselling Author of the Sexy Adult Romance series Bayou Stix.

She attended Southeastern Louisiana University and Louisiana State University where she majored in Mass Communications, centering her studies in Journalism. Unfortunately, life intervened and she never finished her studies.

She lives in small town Louisiana with her husband, two children, and five fur babies.

When she's not chained to her laptop pounding out sexy stories she can usually be found playing 'Supermom', reading, gardening (playing in the dirt), listening to music and dancing like a fool, cooking, baking, crafting, or catching up on her family oriented blog.

She loves to incorporate pieces of Louisiana into her writing.

You can find her here:

Facebook:

www.facebook.com/SkyeTurnerAuthor

Twitter:

@SkyeTurner_Auth

Blog:

www.skyeturnerauthor.com

READER GROUP/ Street Team on Facebook:

Skye Turner's Bayou Belle's and Beau's

www.facebook.com/groups/1425424561003650/

Goodreads:

www.goodreads.com/author/show/7164331.Skye_Turner

E-mail:

skyeturnerauthor@gmail.com

I love hearing from readers, so please feel free to reach out!

Cursed Love

The Cursed Series, #1

By t. h. snyder

Prologue

Sitting Indian style on my twin-sized bed, I fight through the final battle as Zelda on my Nintendo.

I've been trying to beat this game for the past week and now I'm so close. I only have this one life left, I need to do this…I need to win.

With my sword drawn out, my tongue darts over to the side of my mouth and I can feel my heart beating faster through my chest. As my sweaty hands hold on tightly to the controller, my thumbs work their magic to defeat the unsightly creature on my TV screen.

One more spear to the torso should do the trick and I'll be the Zelda legend. A smile forms across my face, and I know very well that I'm about to become 'The Champion'.

My eyes are glued to the colors flying across the screen as I hear my bedroom door creak open.

For just a second, I turn my head to see my mom walking in with my tuxedo in her hands. I roll my eyes and quickly look back to the fight, but it's a moment too late.

"Mom!" I scream.

I toss the controller toward the end of my bed and cross my arms over my chest.

"Lincoln, this is no time to throw a temper tantrum," she says with a serious look on her face. "You're nine years old and you're expected to act like a mature young man."

I look up at her with a pout, "Yes, ma'am."

She nods her head and smiles.

"That's better. Now get yourself off of your bed and get dressed. I'll be back in here in less than thirty minutes and I want you dressed and ready to meet our guests for dinner."

"Yes, ma'am."

I watch as she hangs my tuxedo on the back of my bedroom door and exits the room.

Tonight is one of the biggest nights for our family, not just for my dad. I know I need to act a certain way and be on my best behavior. It's nights like this that I wish I was just a normal kid.

Ever since I can remember I've been told to act like a gentleman, use appropriate manners, not to slouch, and speak up only when spoken to. For a kid my age, it really kinda sucks.

I just wish I was more like my best friend Daulton. He's the luckiest kid I know. His parents let him do whatever he wants, leave the house whenever he wants, and just be a kid.

Not me, I'm a Minzotto. I'll have to do as Mom and Dad say and follow in the political footsteps of my parents. My older brother and sister are already talking about their future careers, but seriously, I'm only nine years old. How the heck am I supposed to know what I want to do when I grow up? As of right now, all I know is that I'd rather play Nintendo than celebrate Dad's election night for another term as congressman of our stupid state.

I slump my shoulders and slide off of my bed. Walking toward my bedroom door, I take off my while polo and reach for the tuxedo shirt. Pulling it off the hanger, I make quick work of getting myself dressed before my mom comes back into my room.

As I'm tying my shoes, I see my bedroom door open out of the corner of my eyes. Mom doesn't say a word while she looks in on me with my brother and sister standing on either side of her.

Mom stands tall next to my siblings and she looks very pretty in her long black dress. Her hair is pulled up off her shoulders and she's wearing a fancy necklace that hangs down to the neckline of her dress.

Shelton, my older brother, is dressed in a similar tuxedo as mine and Mimi, my older sister, is wearing a long shimmery blue dress.

I look down at myself and hope that I appear to be as presentable as them. Standing from my bed, I walk toward my mom. Not a word is spoken nor a glance of my siblings in the wrong direction. I follow them as the four of us walk down the grand staircase leading into the foyer of our home.

As I reach the last few steps, I see my dad walking toward us.

My eyes follow him as he leans forward to place a kiss on Mom's cheek. A smile creeps across her face and his hand goes to the bottom of her back.

Our parents turn to face me, Shelton, and Mimi.

"The guests will be arriving momentarily and dinner will be served promptly at seven. I don't think I need to remind the three of you that this is election night. It's a night to celebrate and enjoy one another as a family; however, I still expect courtesy and manners amongst our guests."

"Yes, sir," Shelton replies.

I tilt my head to the floor and roll my eyes. *Suck up.* My sister nudges my side and I look up to see our father nodding his head as he leads us toward the formal living room.

For what feels like an eternity, I stand around and watch as my parents discuss the evening with guests as they start to arrive.

Collin, Dad's campaign manager, calls for everyone to

move to the dining room for dinner. I take my seat next to Mimi and enjoy the meal our chef has prepared for us.

I find myself gazing off into space, not that it's unusual during these kinds of events. I don't know why it's so important for me to even be here. My parents haven't looked at or spoken to me since I came down the stairs. To be honest, I don't know that they'd even miss me if I slipped out of the room and upstairs to play Nintendo.

The idea of leaving piques my interest more and more as the conversations begin to turn toward the polls. I'm so bored I can't help but yawn as I look around the table at all the men and women here to support the election tonight.

I plot my plan in my head for the next few minutes. Daulton only lives about two miles over the bridge. If I leave after dinner, I should be able to make it to his house in less than fifteen minutes.

My mind is made up—as soon as dinner is over, I'm ditching out of here.

I may only be a nine-year-old boy, but I sure as heck

know that I'm not needed here tonight.

Once we're excused from the table, I watch as everyone moves into the other rooms and I quickly make my escape through the open garage door.

I can feel the sweat trickle down my back the faster I pedal my bike. In a few minutes I should be at Daulton's house; I just hope he's home.

Rounding the last turn in his neighborhood, I see that the front porch light is on and the garage door is open with his mom's car parked inside.

I hop off of my bike and lean it against the side of the house. As I march my way up onto the front porch, I take off my jacket and hang it across my arm. I reach for the doorbell and wait for someone to come and answer the door.

The front door swings open and Daulton stands in the doorway wearing a Skate or Die tee-shirt and black running pants.

A smile comes across his face as he pushes open the screen door.

"Dude, what are you doing here? Isn't it like election night or something?" he asks, standing up against the door frame with his arms crossed in front of his chest.

I look to him and punch him in the shoulder.

"Yeah, it's something alright. I was bored out of my mind and needed to get out of there fast."

"Linc, your parents are going to kill you. Are you sure you should be here?"

"I'm sure, now let me in and let's play some video games."

I make my way through the door and follow Daulton back to his room.

The house is eerily quiet and dark. I know his mom is here, I saw her car parked in the garage. It's really no bother to me, so I shrug it off and plop myself down on one of the bean bag chairs in front of the TV.

Daulton loads a game into the Nintendo and hands me a controller. For the next hour or so we battle one another, each of us winning a game or two.

Lights flash across his bedroom wall from the outside and I hear a car door slam.

My ear perks to a noise coming from the front yard. It sounds like someone's yelling, but I can't make it out.

Daulton grabs my hand and I follow him into the other room.

He quickly closes the old, cracked, wooden closet door after us and we slide back to the wall behind the musty clothes and boxes.

My body is trembling and I can hear Daulton's teeth chattering in fear.

What the heck just happened?

All I remember is playing video games in his bedroom and before I know it, he's pulling me into the guest room closet.

I follow his lead, completely clueless as to what's going

on. A million thoughts are racing through my head.

Is it his mom? His dad?

Is there a robber in the house and we're hiding so that he doesn't find us?

Is there a chance that something bad is going to happen and I'll never make it home to see my family again?

Daulton and I have been best friends since Kindergarten. We've played tee-ball together and even made the traveling baseball team this year. The two of us have been inseparable since we first met.

He's the one friend I can get along with and be myself. I don't have to pretend around him, and I sure as heck don't have to act like a congressman's son when we're together.

No matter how badly we mess around or bully one another on the playground, I always know I'm safe with him...that is, until now.

I rest my head in my hands and can feel the tears prick the back of my eyelids. I never should have snuck out of home and ridden my bike to Daulton's house tonight. It was a big mistake and now I'm scared to death to be here with him.

When my parents find out that I'm gone, I'll be in more trouble than ever before. But one thing is for sure, being grounded for life is better than hiding in this closet.

A door slams in the other room and I hear a muffled cry. Three loud sounds vibrate the wall behind us and I can only imagine what could be causing the thumping noise.

Our bodies both jump at the clamor coming from outside the closet. I hear his mother's scream and the sound of something slamming into the wall.

Daulton moves his body further back into the closet and I look in his direction. All I see is pitch black except for the subtle light coming through the space between the bottom of the door and the floor.

Sounds echo from the other room and more shouts and screams follow. I can't make out what's happening, but the fear coursing through my body tells me that something isn't right in this house.

A loud bang goes off…and then another. Daulton reaches his hand out to me and our bodies shiver together.

Moments pass by—I'm not sure if it's seconds or minutes—but it feels like a lifetime.

The front door slams shut and I can feel my heart pounding through my tuxedo shirt.

This has to be the worst night of my life and I can only imagine what's going to happen next.

Made in the USA
San Bernardino, CA
10 December 2014